S0-AKC-610

CHILLER THRILLERS™

THE SECRET OF SPIDER MOTEL

WRITTEN BY MEL GILDEN   ILLUSTRATED BY DAVID ROE

Reader's Digest
Children's Books®

New York, New York • Montréal, Québec • Bath, United Kingdom

Story by Mel Gilden
Illustrated by David Roe
Cover Painted by Thomas Mason

Published by Reader's Digest Children's Books
44 South Broadway, White Plains, NY, 10601 U.S.A. and
Reader's Digest Children's Publishing Limited,
The Ice House, 124-126 Walcot Street, Bath UK BA1 5BG
© 2012 Reader's Digest Children's Publishing, Inc.
Original copyright © 2002. All rights reserved. Reader's Digest and
Reader's Digest Children's Books are registered trademarks
of The Reader's Digest Association, Inc.
Manufactured in China.
10 9 8 7 6 5 4 3 2 1
LPP/04/12

CONTENTS

CHAPTER ONE

PLENTY OF NOTHING

It had already been a long trip, and we weren't even half done. We were supposed to be on a family vacation, but personally I would rather have stayed in the backyard cooling off under the sprinkler, eating an Eskimo Pie, and reading a science fiction novel from the library.

Some of the stuff we'd seen was actually pretty spectacular—the Grand Canyon and Hoover Dam, for instance. No matter how big I thought they were going to be, they were bigger than that. No, even bigger than that!

I was sitting in the backseat of the car with my little brother, Rocky, trying not to melt in the heat. My father explained that the heat wouldn't bother us because it was a dry heat. My mother was of the opinion that it didn't matter how moist the heat was; when it got to be too hot, it was too hot. I agreed with her.

For the past hundred miles or so there hadn't been much to see out the window except sand, scraggly cactus, and the shimmer that rose from hot rocks. Even other cars were rare. It was easy to pretend we were rolling along a road on another planet—one without bathrooms, gas stations, or convenience stores.

All of us were hungry and tired. Rocky and I were also bored with the coloring books, puzzles, and games with which Mom had stocked the backseat. There was nothing left to do but fight.

"Mom," I called out, "Rocky is on my side of the seat again."

"I am not," Rocky yelled in protest. Six-year-olds!

"Are too," I argued.

"Am not," Rocky complained.

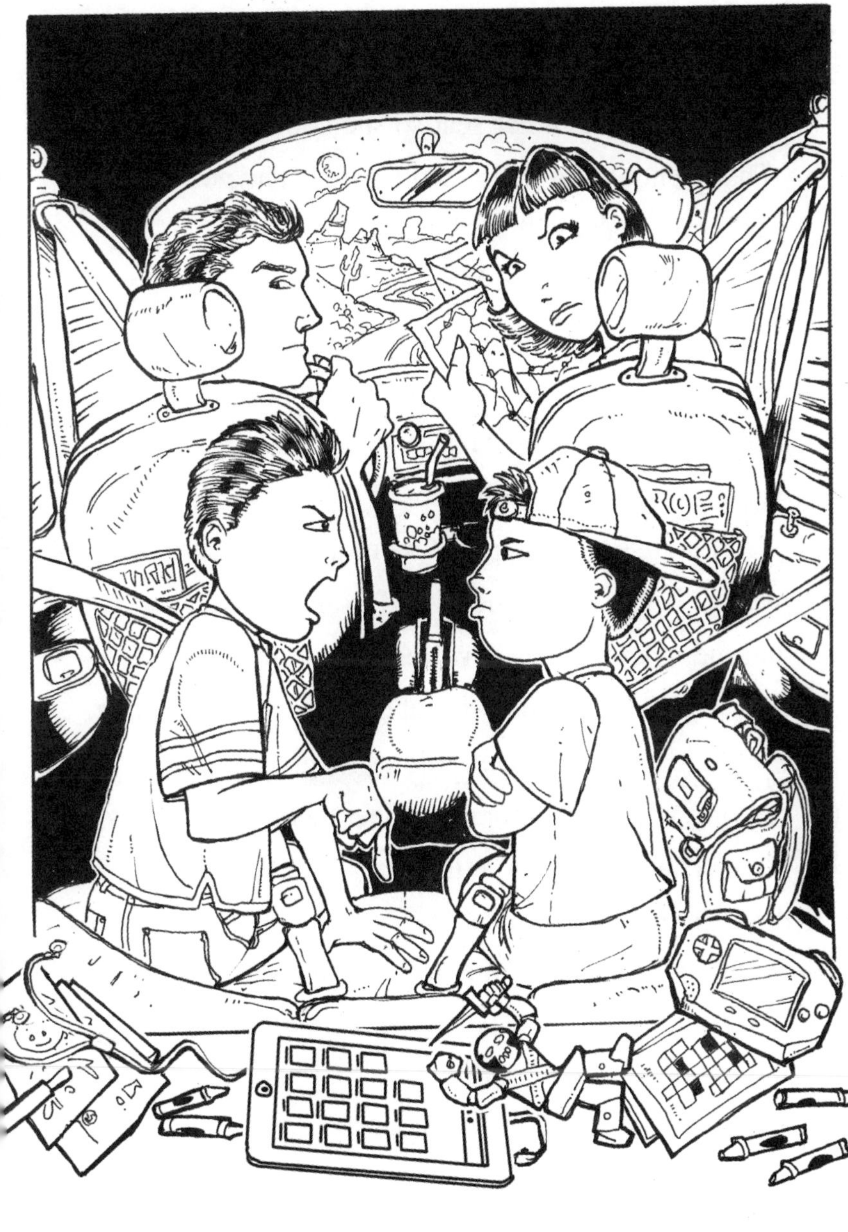

"Too."

"Not."

Mom turned in her seat so she could glare at us. "That's enough of that," Mom said. "The next one of you who speaks will walk home."

Even Rocky rolled his eyes. Mom occasionally grounded us or wouldn't let us have dessert or turned off the TV early, but she had never made good on a threat of this kind. Our parents weren't bad.

"Sure, Mom." I said.

Of course, for the past few miles Mom and Dad had not been setting such good examples for Rocky and me. "Are you sure we're going in the right direction?" Mom asked for about the hundredth time.

"Yes, I'm sure," Dad said as he gripped the steering wheel even tighter. "See, there's the sun over there. That means we're traveling east. You're holding the map upside down."

"Keep your eyes on the road, Buster," Mom said. "Shouldn't we be in Phoenix by now?"

"We're making good time," Dad assured her.

"I'm hungry," Rocky cried. This was not exactly

news. None of us had eaten for hours.

"We'll eat when we get to Phoenix," Dad said.

"Should that ever actually happen," Mom added.

Dad gave her a dirty look.

Something clanged against the bottom of the car.

"What was that?" I asked.

"I don't know," Rocky said.

"I don't know either," Mom said. "Dear, maybe we'd better stop and take a look."

"Just a rock," Dad said. "I thought you wanted to get to Phoenix."

"I do," Mom replied, in a way that was loaded with meaning.

Dad sighed and slowed to pull off the road. I don't know why he bothered to pull over. Looking through the back window, I didn't see another car all the way to where the road disappeared in the bright haze.

We stopped in the gravel by the side of the road and all got out of the car. Who knew when we'd have another chance to stretch? While Mom and Dad checked the car, Rocky and I stared out into the desert.

"Wow," Rocky commented.

"Yeah," I said. "I've never seen so much nothing in my life." The sighing wind seemed to pick up our voices and carry them away.

Mom handed Dad a pair of work gloves from the glove compartment, and he got down on his hands and knees to look under the car. "Yeow," he cried. "Even through the gloves the pavement is hot enough to fry an egg."

"Good one, Dad," I said.

"Thanks," he said, and bent down to look under the car again.

"See anything?" Mom asked.

"Just the bottom of the car," Dad said as he got to his feet. "Besides, even if something was wrong, I wouldn't be able to fix it out here."

"If somebody had remembered to charge the cell phone batteries—"

Dad interrupted her. "Don't start with me, Marge," he said. "All right, guys," he shouted. His voice sounded thin and weird in the blistering hot air. "Pile in. Phoenix isn't going to come to us."

We all got back into the car. I think we were

all relieved when Dad was actually able to start the engine. As we rolled out onto the highway I noticed that the short rest stop made me feel better.

"I'm sorry I was on your side," Rocky said.

"That's okay," I replied.

The stop had done us all a lot of good.

"What's that rubbing noise?" Mom asked.

"I don't know," Dad said. He leaned closer to the dashboard so he could hear the engine better.

The rubbing noise came faster, and soon it was more of a squeal.

"Are we gonna die?" Rocky asked quietly.

It wasn't such a weird question, I thought. If nowhere had a middle, this was it. I could already feel my throat shriveling up, even though I'd just had a cup of water from the cooler.

"We're not going to die," Mom assured him.

We were still moving, but to the squeal was added a sort of a knock, and a few minutes later an occasional cough. I couldn't see any red lights on the dashboard, but the engine didn't sound good to me.

"What's the next town?" Dad asked, his voice a

little frantic.

"I'm hoping it's Phoenix," Mom said. "But you never know."

"Right."

The car continued to roll along, but the engine sounded worse.

"What's that?" Dad asked.

"What?" Mom replied.

"That, there," Dad said, and pointed out the windshield. Something wavered in the heat a few miles down the road.

"Looks like a building," Mom said.

"Who would want to live way out here?" I asked.

"Bad guys?" Rocky suggested. "Weird aliens?"

"You've been watching too much TV," I said. But as we approached the building, I could not help fearing that my brother might be right.

"Hang on, kids." Dad said. "We're going in!"

CHAPTER TWO

*T*he two-story building was U-shaped, with the open part facing the road. Next to it was a smaller building identified as SPIDER CAFÉ in faded letters. A big weatherworn sign at the top of a tall pole in the middle of the empty parking lot said SPIDER ROADSIDE ATTRACTION AND MOTOR HOTEL. Swinging from a single chain was a smaller sign that said VACANCY. I could believe that—the parking lot was empty except for our car and little ripples of sand.

The building was rundown. The paint on its walls may have been a real color once, but the wind and the sun had done their work and it was now a grayish-brownish yellow—not so much a color as a sickness. Some of the doors were splintered in spots.

The car gave a last gasp at the edge of the parking lot. While Mom steered, Dad put on his gloves again and pushed the car to a door with the word OFFICE on it.

"Stay here," Dad said. While he walked to the office door and tried the knob, the rest of us got out of the car, too. Not even Mom objected. She joined Dad at the office door. It seemed to be locked.

"We're going to look around," I said.

"Don't get lost," Mom called. "We don't know what's lurking around here." She rapped on the door with her knuckles.

"Snakes, do you think?" Rocky whispered as we wandered off.

"I heard that," Mom called. "If you see a snake, you are to come back here immediately."

"Okay, Mom," I said.

Nobody had opened the office door yet, and Mom and Dad were now whispering to each other furiously.

Rocky and I walked along the front of the building trying doorknobs and looking into the windows of all the rooms. All the doors were locked and each window was blocked by a heavy curtain.

We climbed the stairs to the second-floor walkway and looked out into the desert. In the setting sun, the desert was kind of pretty—pink and purple, and deep blue shadows. But I was too hot and sweaty to enjoy it.

"Are we going to die out here in the desert?" Rocky asked again.

"Of course not," I said with a snort. I hoped I sounded convincing. "Dad'll get the car started and we'll be on our way to Phoenix again."

"But what if he can't get it started?"

"Then somebody will come along and help us."

"I don't think people come here often. It looks like a ghost town."

"You mean a ghost motel," I said.

"Whatever!" Rocky cried as he threw up his hands. "We're doomed!"

"Okay, fine. Have it your way." A chilly wind blew off the desert, and I shivered. I went back downstairs and I could hear Rocky clomping down the stairs behind me. I went back to the car. Mom and Dad had the hood up and they were staring at the engine. They looked discouraged.

"Rocky thinks we're going to die," I reported.

"So what else is new?" Dad asked.

"We may be stuck," Mom said. "There's no one around."

"Don't let Rocky hear you say that," I said. "He'll never stop whining."

"Don't let Rocky hear you say what?" Rocky asked as he walked up.

"No ice cream tonight," Dad said.

Rocky looked confused. "I wasn't expecting ice cream."

"See how things work out?" Dad said.

Rocky was still confused, but at least he didn't make a fuss. I guessed that Rocky was trying to figure out what Dad meant, and it was taking his mind off his fears.

"What's wrong with the car?" I asked.

"Grit in the fuel line," Dad said. His idea sounded more like a suggestion than a statement of fact.

"Gremlins," Mom said.

"Huh?" Rocky inquired.

"During World War II when anything went wrong with an airplane," Dad explained, "the pilots said that nasty little elf creatures, called gremlins, were responsible."

Rocky's eyes got big.

Mom sighed. "It was just a joke," she said.

Nobody laughed.

"Maybe it really is grit in the fuel line," Dad said. He walked to the back of the car and opened the trunk. After rummaging inside for a moment, he came up with a small tool kit. He carried it to the front of the car as if he was going to do something with it, but he only set the kit on the ground and stared glumly at the engine again.

"Is there anything left to eat?" I asked.

"There are crackers and peanut butter in the cooler," Mom said. "Help yourself."

"No, thanks," I said. "I'm not hungry enough yet." Who packs crackers and peanut butter for a trip across the desert? "Can we check out the Spider Café?"

"We'll try later, after your Dad fixes the car."

That meant no food for the near future, but I didn't say a thing. By this time it was getting dark and the air had turned pretty cold. I was surprised that the desert wasn't hot all the time. Mom got her sweater, and Rocky and I pulled our jackets from the trunk. Dad didn't seem to notice. He was still staring at the engine.

"Are we going to stay here tonight?" Rocky asked.

Mom glanced at Dad, who still hadn't moved. "Well, sure," she said, as she attempted a smile. "It'll be fun. Better than sleeping in the car."

"But the doors to all the rooms are locked."

"Motel rooms usually are. But if no one is here, then we'll just have to force open one of the doors."

"Is that legal?" I asked.

"Don't argue with your mother," Dad said. "Desperate people have to do desperate things."

"Are we really desperate?" I asked.

"Soon, maybe. I'll let you know. So far, this is just an adventure."

Rocky and I nodded.

Having nothing better to do, we strolled around the

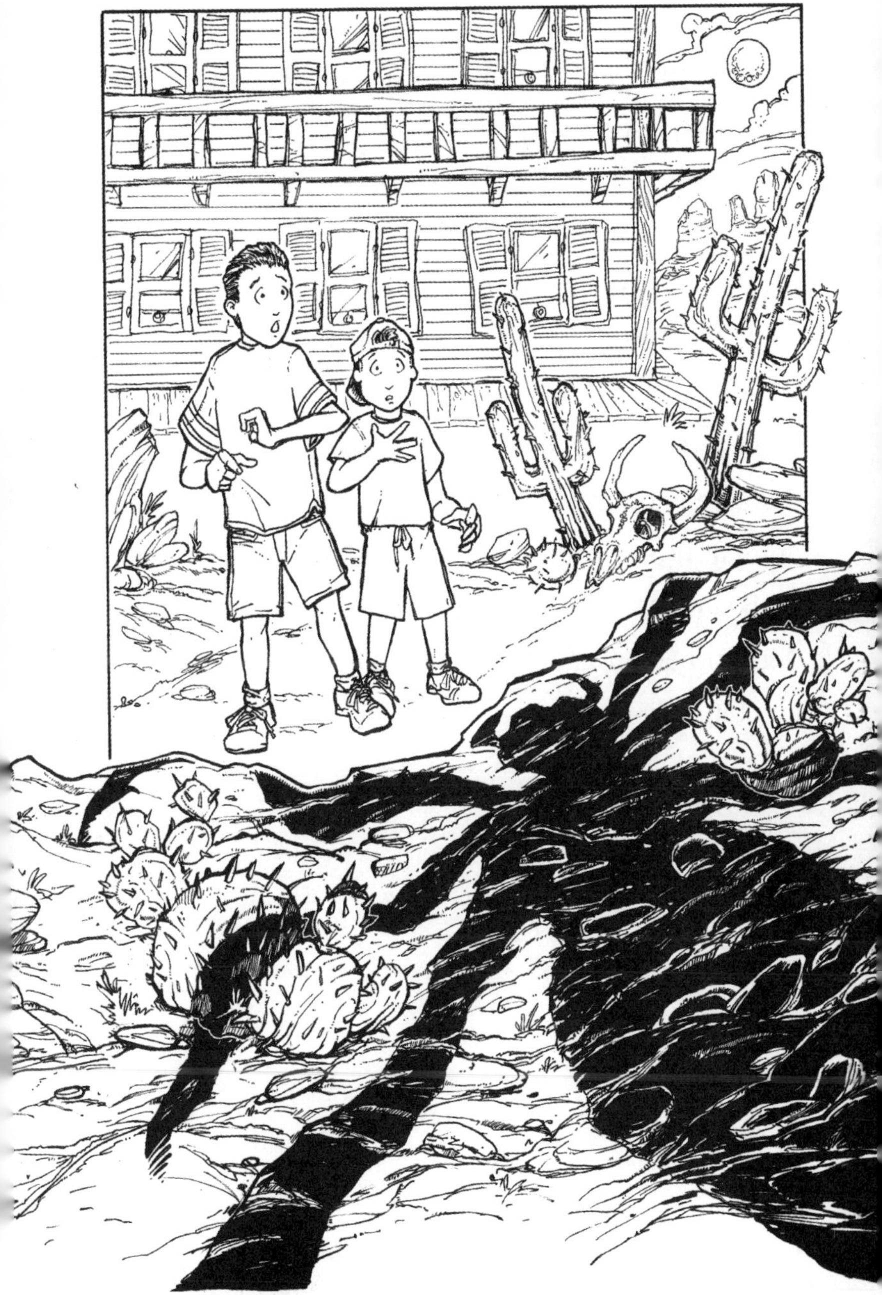

side of the U-shaped building. It was pretty much the same as the front. Along the back of the building were windows, but no doors.

"What's that?" Rocky asked, pointing at what seemed to be a light burning in a small building off by itself behind the main motel.

"Gremlins?" I suggested and walked along a driveway toward the light with Rocky in tow. Maybe somebody was around after all. The light went out and the garage door went down squealing like a wounded animal; it hit the ground with a boom. We watched with surprise as the creature that lowered the garage door turned around and saw us for the first time. It was a giant spider.

CHAPTER THREE

RAGGS MOPPIT

Actually, it wasn't a giant spider. It was a tall, skinny man in a rubber spider suit. He had a long, thin face and an enormous Adam's apple jutting from his neck. The arms and legs of his suit—including two extra rubbery spider legs that drooped unconvincingly from either side of his body—were made to look hairy and segmented, like real spider legs. The man and his spider suit seemed made for each other. Rocky and I stared at the man while he stared at us. For a long time nobody moved.

"May I help you?" the man asked.

"I'm Buzz and he's Rocky. Our car broke down."

"Your car broke down?"

"Our parents' car," Rocky said. "Why are you wearing that suit?"

The man didn't seem bothered by Rocky's question. "It's kind of like advertising," the man said. "You know, a Spider Roadside Attraction and Motor Hotel run by a spider?" His laugh encouraged us to laugh with him. I managed a smile. Rocky just gawked. "Besides," the man went on, "I think I look rather dapper in it. Don't you?"

"Sure," Rocky and I agreed together. I was pretty sure Rocky didn't know what dapper meant.

"Are you planning to stay the night?" the man asked politely. "We have a wonderful vacation package on special right now. And the food at the Spider Café is very good."

"You'll have to ask our parents," I said, though I was sure they would say yes. It was either that or have crackers and peanut butter for dinner and spend the night in the car.

We led the man back around the building and found Mom aiming a flashlight at the engine for Dad, who at that moment said a very bad word. He backed away from the car, shaking one greasy hand.

"Mom!" I cried. "Dad! This is Mr...." I realized that I didn't know the man's name.

"The name is Moppit," he said, smiling. "Raggs

Moppit."

"I'm Buster Flebius," Dad said, "and this is my wife, Marge."

"Charmed," Mr. Moppit said sincerely. "Are you folks interested in a room or two?"

"We are," Dad said. "But we won't pay more than your regular rates."

Mr. Moppit seemed shocked. "I wasn't thinking of charging you that much," he said. "After all, it's the off-season."

"That's fine, then," Dad said agreeably. "I don't suppose you fix cars, too?"

"Not officially," Mr. Moppit said. "But I'd be delighted to take a look at your car in the morning. Come on in and sign the register."

Mr. Moppit unlocked the office door and invited Dad inside.

"Imagine finding a man in a spider suit way out here," Mom said.

"Where'd you expect to find a man in a spider suit?" Rocky asked.

Mom shrugged. "I hope that restaurant is open,"

she said.

"It is. Mr. Moppit said so," I put in.

"Anything would be better than crackers and peanut butter," Mom replied, and ruffled my hair.

A few minutes later Dad came out of the room looking pretty pleased. He carried a couple of keys, each attached to a big square piece of green plastic.

"What a weird guy," Dad said.

"He's in a spider suit," said Mom. "You mean, weirder than that?"

"Well, it's obvious no one's here except us, but he made a big show of making sure rooms were empty before he offered them to us. When I asked him what the problem was, he acted awfully secretive. I wonder what's in those other rooms, the rooms we're not going to be in."

"Counterfeit money?" Mom suggested. "Dead bodies?"

"Maybe," Dad said with a smile, "the maid just hasn't been in."

"You're probably right."

But inside I wasn't so sure.

"Okay, guys," Dad said in his most enthusiastic voice. "Let's get settled. Mr. Moppit says he'll meet us in the Spider Café in a few minutes."

Mr. Moppit said that since he had some vacancies just at the moment (hah!), he'd give us two rooms at a bargain rate. Mom and Dad were staying in room eight and I was staying with Rocky in room seven. We carried our stuff to the rooms, which were exactly the same. Each contained two beds and a small bathroom. There was some other furniture and a telephone. The television was the size of a washing machine and had a small, round screen like a porthole on a ship. When I turned it on, all I saw was snow. I picked up the telephone receiver and heard nothing, not even a dial tone. The deadness sounded strange in my ear. The rooms looked tidy, but they smelled really old and dusty. I think we were the first people to stay in them for a long time.

After we put our stuff away in the closets and went to the bathroom, I tried opening the windows. The window in the bathroom was easy to open, but the one in the front, next to the door, didn't even have a handle. After Rocky and I jumped on the beds for a while, we met our parents outside and walked to the Spider Café.

"Your father is quite a negotiator," Mom said. "He got us each of these rooms for ten bucks a night."

"Wow," Rocky and I said. Ten bucks sounded like a lot of money for a room, but what did I know?

Over the door was a wooden cutout of a large spider. Inside, the café was bright and cheery, and it was much warmer than the desert at night. Noise and good-food smells came from the kitchen.

Dad sat us down in a booth.

"No, no!" Mr. Moppit exclaimed when he emerged from the kitchen and saw us. He was wearing one of those big chef's hats, and over his spider suit he wore a long apron that said LET'S EAT! on the front. "I'm afraid my waitstaff is off tonight. You'll have to sit at the counter so I can serve you myself. It's more friendly that way, don't you agree?"

Dad glanced at Mom and she glanced back. You could tell they weren't used to having the cook order the patrons around. But they got up, and Rocky and I

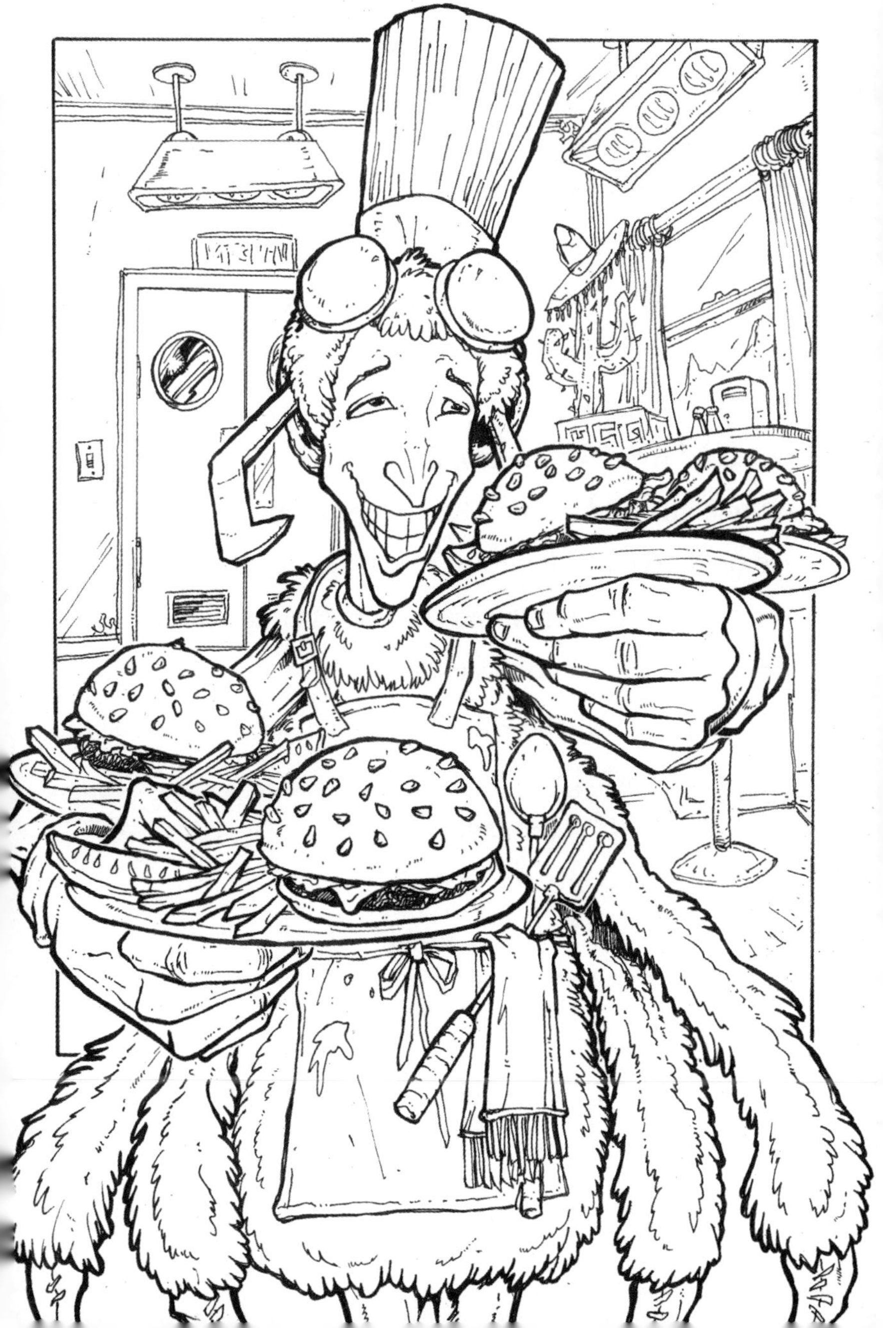

followed them to the counter.

Mr. Moppit quickly doled out paper napkins and silverware. In another moment, each of us had a glass of ice water, which we polished off pretty quickly. Mr. Moppit immediately brought out a big sweating pitcher with which he refilled our glasses.

"I don't see a menu, do you?" Dad said.

Mom was about to reply when Mr. Moppit emerged from the kitchen carrying two plates of food on one arm and another two plates on the other arm. He put one plate down in front of each of us. Each plate held the same thing: a hamburger and a pile of fries and a quarter of a pickle.

"How do you know this is what I want?" Mom asked.

"Isn't it what you want?"

"Well, yes," Mom admitted.

"There you are, then."

Dad nodded. "You're good," he said. "You're really good."

I didn't know whether Mr. Moppit was a mind reader or just a good guesser, but the food was terrific. It turned out to be exactly what I wanted, too. Even

Rocky, who is pretty finicky, wolfed it down. When I was done, I didn't have much room left. Then Mr. Moppit set a hot fudge sundae in front of me. I made room.

"Does this come with our dinner?" Dad asked, looking at the sundae.

Mr. Moppit assured him that it did.

After we finished, we sat at the counter in what Dad calls "anaconda mode"—just feeling good and digesting.

"Would you like to see the roadside attraction now?" Mr. Moppit asked.

Rocky and I nodded enthusiastically.

Mom burped delicately. "Actually," she said, "it's been a difficult day. I know I'm ready for bed."

"It won't take long," Mr. Moppit said. "And I'm sure you'll find the roadside attraction illuminating and educational." He winked at Rocky and me. He was right. Parents can't resist anything educational. Dad finally agreed to take a look. Mr. Moppit led us outside and into the building next door.

"This'll be great!" I told Rocky.

CHAPTER FOUR

THE ROADSIDE ATTRACTION

The building next door to the Spider Café was the Spider Roadside Attraction. Mr. Moppit jangled a ring of keys as he unlocked the door and shooed us inside. A cold wind had come up, so we were all pretty glad to be indoors again.

Mr. Moppit flicked a switch near the door. Fluorescent lights blinked on and began to buzz.

The roadside attraction was a big square room with glass display cases down the center and a big metal cabinet in one corner. Small photographs of the desert that looked as if they'd been pulled from calendars (complete with a row of torn holes across the bottom of each one) were taped to the walls. The place looked kind of cheap and grungy.

"Welcome, welcome," Mr. Moppit called, as if he were talking to a much larger group. He went on in a quieter voice. "I usually charge a buck a head to get in here, but what the heck." We were huddled near the door. "Come in," Mr. Moppit cried. "Look around! Be amazed!"

Mom and Dad walked off in one direction, and Rocky and I walked off in another. Mr. Moppit stood near the door, smiling. The only thing that amazed me was that Mr. Moppit could charge even a buck to see the Spider Roadside Attraction. It was certainly one of the lamest collections of junk in the world.

I saw a stuffed two-headed snake, which might have been interesting except that one of the heads was obviously sewn on. Nearby was a jackalope. I'd seen joke pictures of these—using photographic tricks to give a jackrabbit antlers. Instead of regular antlers, the jackalope at the Spider Roadside Attraction had one of those TV antennas some people have on top of their TV to improve reception. It was tied on with red wire.

There was a cactus that looked like Darth Vader if you squinted, a bullet said to have been fired by Billy the Kid, a big rock and seven little rocks that were supposed to look like Snow White and the Seven

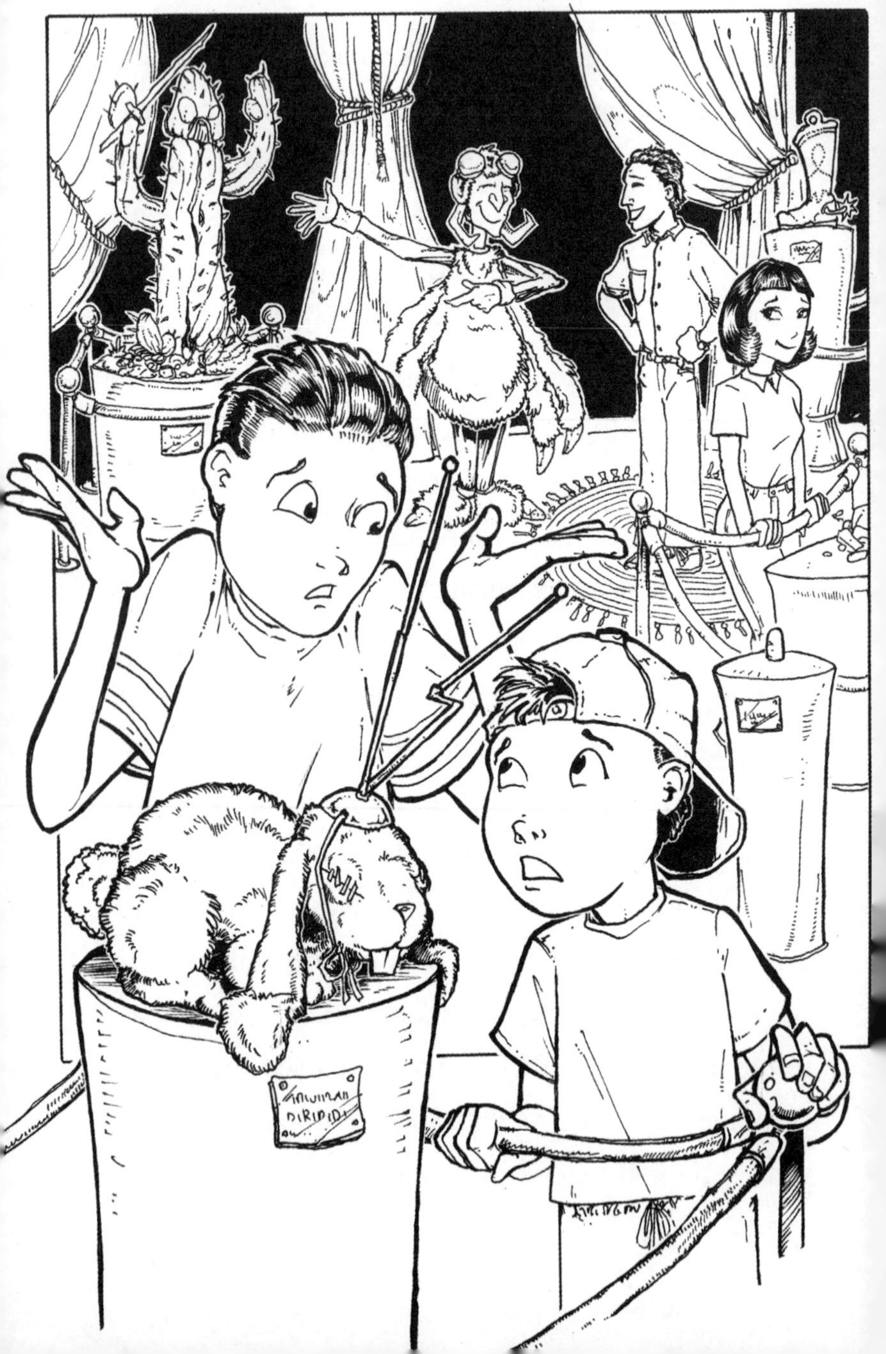

Dwarfs, and a pile of sand that was supposed to have come from Monument Valley, where a lot of movies had been made.

Each item had a card in front of it that explained the display. Good thing, too, because some of the exhibits, like Snow White and the Seven Dwarfs, were just rocks or dirt that looked a lot like the rocks and dirt available by the acre outside. Even so, most of the cards didn't help much. The card in front of Snow White and the dwarfs said, IS TALE FROM FAIRIES ABOUT SNOW WHITE, SEVEN SMALL PEOPLE INCLUDED. Entertaining, maybe even funny, but not very helpful. A few of the exhibits were missing and replaced by cards that said WE'LL BE BACK SOON!

"What do you think?" Rocky whispered.

"What a load of junk!" I said.

"Yeah." He looked around with contempt.

We strolled back to the door where Mr. Moppit was waiting. Mom and Dad were already there. Mr. Moppit looked a little disappointed.

"You don't seem quite as amazed as I thought you'd be," he said.

"It is amazing stuff," Dad assured him. "But we've had a long day. We're just too bushed to appreciate what you have here."

"Maybe tomorrow," Mom added.

"Of course," Mr. Moppit said. He seemed to buy the explanation Mom and Dad sold him. Not even Rocky believed it.

"Time for bed," Dad said. He smiled at Mr. Moppit. "And thanks for all your kindness. We'll see you in the morning, before we leave."

"Assuming we leave at all," Mom said under her breath.

Mr. Moppit led us through the cold outside air to our rooms. He stood around making everybody nervous while Mom and Dad made sure Rocky and I were settled.

"We'll be fine," I said, with annoyance. What was the big deal? There were two beds in the room and we knew the bathroom worked. Each of us had flushed the toilet a couple of times just to make sure.

"Take good care of your little brother," Mom said to me. "We'll be right next door if you need us."

"They can handle it," Dad said, and punched me in the shoulder. Then they kissed us good night, which was a little embarrassing in front of Mr. Moppit, and they all left.

We got undressed and put on our pajamas and brushed our teeth. We settled down in our beds, and I reached over to turn out the big lamp on the table between us. The room was suddenly really dark.

"What do you think, Buzz?" Rocky asked.

"About what?"

"You know. Do you think we'll be able to leave in the morning?"

"I hope so," I said. "I don't want to become one of Mr. Moppit's exhibits. You know: 'FOUR PERSONS IN AUTOMOBILE HAVING BROKEN PARTS SEE NOWHERE.'"

Rocky giggled and then sighed. "I don't want to turn out like that either."

I listened to Mom and Dad talking in the next room. I couldn't make out the words, but their voices made me feel comfortable. Pretty soon I drifted off to sleep.

Next thing I knew I was awakened by the strangest noises I'd ever heard.

CHAPTER Five

NIGHT iN THE DESERT

I lay there for a while, blinking in the darkness and waiting for the noises to happen again. A few minutes later they did. First there was banging, and then a sound like big sparks crackling, and finally the loud squeal of metal on metal.

"Buzz?" Rocky whispered loudly. "You awake?"

"Yeah. Did you hear those noises?"

"Yeah. I'm afraid."

A few minutes later the noises hadn't stopped. "I want to go see what they are," I whispered. "Do you want to come?"

"No."

"Well, I'm going."

"You can't leave me here! Mom told you to take care of me."

"Then you'd better come."

We argued like that for a while. At last I got out of bed and put on my clothes. When he saw I was serious about investigating, Rocky did the same. "Wait for me," he said with a grumble.

I didn't have to wait long. A few minutes later he was dressed. I opened the door, and we slipped out into the night to take a look.

We stood in front of our room for a moment to listen. There were no lights anywhere, not even in our parents' room.

"Look at that," I said, and pointed at the sky.

"Wow!"

We live in a big city. Even when the sky isn't full of clouds, which it usually is, the lights of the city make the stars difficult to see. We can see the Moon, of course, and sometimes we can make out Orion, but that's usually about it.

Out here in the middle of the desert, the sky was a lot more amazing than Mr. Moppit's roadside attraction. It was full of zillions of stars. There were so many that I wouldn't have been able to find the famous constellations even if I remembered what they look like. And the sky between the stars was absolutely black, not gray the way it is in the big city. The night was so dark and the sky was so clear, I could even see wispy clouds and a long white smudge that I knew must be the Milky Way.

The noises came again. They sounded as if they came from around back—maybe from the garage where we'd first met Mr. Moppit.

"Are you sure you want to do this?" Rocky asked. His face looked pale and strained in the starlight.

"Absolutely." I walked along the row of rooms. He followed.

Except for the strange noises and the sound of our footsteps, the night was absolutely silent. I could even hear Rocky and myself breathing.

And that was strange too. I had always heard that the desert was full of life—coyotes, and birds, and lizards, and insects—and that a lot of them were most active at night, hunting and stuff. The silence was a little creepy. Where was everything? Were the animals hiding? Was it their night off? Had aliens abducted all of them? I knew better than to share my thoughts with Rocky. He was weirded out enough already.

We walked to the end of the main motel building. Around the corner was the long driveway, and at the end of that, the mysterious garage.

"Let's go back," Rocky said. He sounded really scared now.

I was a little scared, too, but I was even more curious. "Don't you want to find out what's going on?"

"No. It's none of our beeswax." Rocky turned around and actually took a few steps back toward the room. But when he saw I wasn't coming with him he returned. "If I'm killed in some horrible way, Mom and Dad will never forgive you."

"Nothing's going to kill you," I assured him. I couldn't let on that I was worried, too.

We walked along the driveway with the building on one side and the big, dark, cold emptiness of the desert on the other. The noises continued, growing louder as we approached the garage. A light was on in the garage, just as it had been earlier.

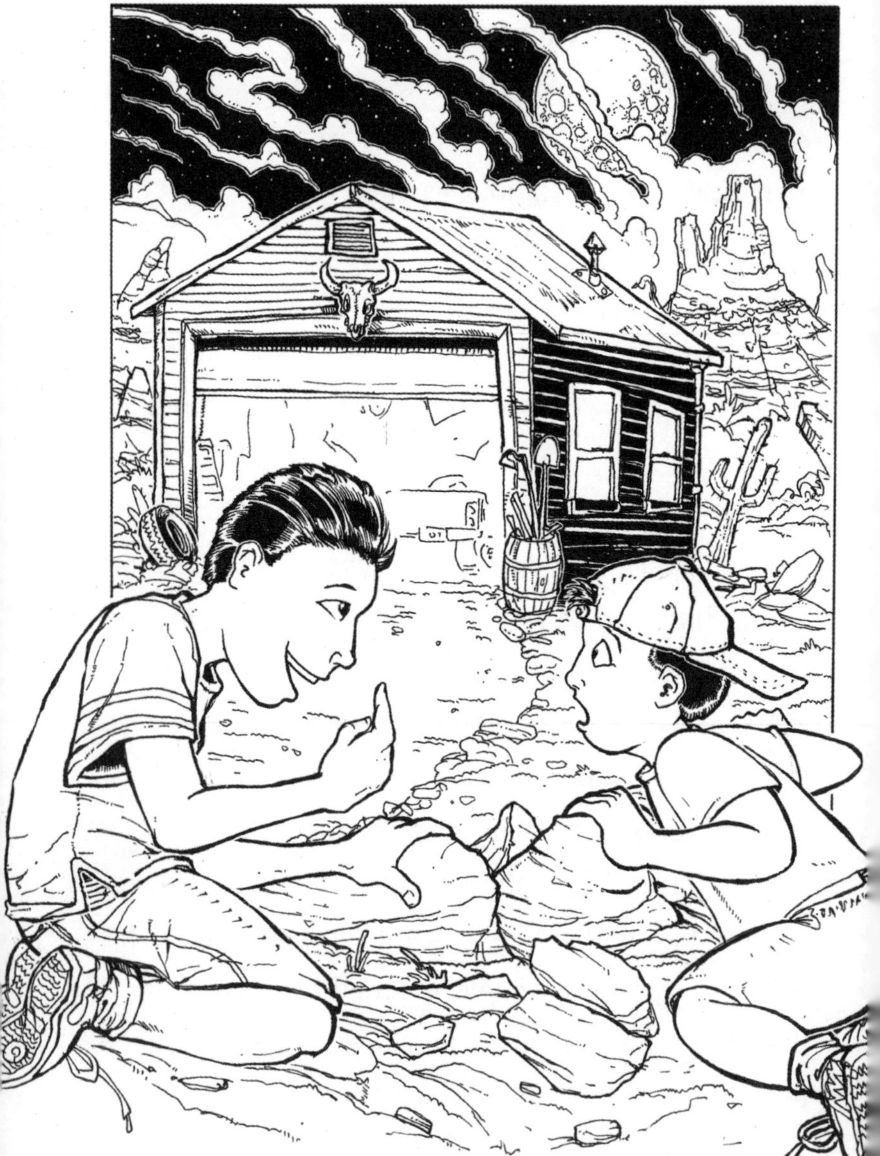

"Maybe Mr. Moppit is fixing our car," Rocky suggested brightly. "He said he would give it a try."

"Our car is out front," I reminded Rocky.

"Unless he pushed it over here after we all went to bed," Rocky said.

"Possible, I guess." But I didn't think so. I thought that whatever was going on had nothing to do with us or our car.

Carefully, we tiptoed up to the garage. It was lit by a single bulb in the ceiling, which cast thick shadows behind everything. What we saw made me sorry I hadn't stayed in my motel room.

It was Mr. Moppit, still dressed as a spider. He seemed to be operating on a dark, man-size lump on the floor of the garage.

CHAPTER SIX

IN THE GARAGE

I clamped my hand on Rocky's shoulder to prevent him from running away. I didn't want to be there all alone. I didn't want to be there at all. Mr. Moppit must have heard us gasp, because he turned around suddenly.

"Hey, boys," he said pleasantly. "Come see what I have here."

I knew that a normal grown-up would have asked us what we were doing up at this hour. The fact that he didn't—plus the fact that he always wore a spider suit and that he knew what people wanted for dinner before they knew it themselves—made me afraid of him. Even though he hadn't actually done anything frightening.

Rocky and I each took a few steps into the garage. It was crowded with tools and oddly formed metal parts. On the shelves were boxes marked with strange symbols. Alien writing? The whole place smelled a little sour and rancid—as if something had gone bad. In his hand Mr. Moppit held a big wrench.

"Come closer, boys," Mr. Moppit said. "I don't bite."

We inched forward until we could see that Mr. Moppit was working on a machine. But it was definitely not of this earth. It was a solid silver thing that seemed to fade around the edges like a clump of mist. It had funny fins and knobs on it, and a hole with blinking lights inside. All in all, it didn't look quite real. Yet there it was. Mr. Moppit watched us as if he'd asked us a question and awaited an answer.

"What is it?" Rocky asked, a little breathless.

"Actually, I have no idea," Mr. Moppit said. "I call it an interociter, which is a word I got from a movie I saw when I was about your age."

"Where did you get it?" I asked.

"The machine? That's a long story." Mr. Moppit set the wrench on the cement floor and sat down on the interociter as if it were just a big rock. "You'd better sit down." He gestured to a couple of stools next to a workbench littered with wires and electronic bits.

"A few years ago I came in off the desert just as you and your parents did today," Mr. Moppit began. "I was tired of living in the city, and I was looking for a place to get away from it all. You understand?"

I had no idea what he was talking about, but I nodded.

"The people who ran the Spider Roadside Attraction and Motor Hotel were nice, but they seemed a little strange. All of them were over six feet tall, and they were thin as string beans. And in bright sunlight their skin looked a little green."

"Were they aliens?" Rocky asked eagerly

Mr. Moppit looked at Rocky with surprise. "Why, how clever of you!" he said delightedly. "It took me a few weeks to make the same guess. They were scientists who came to Earth to collect specimens they could study on their home planet. Some of the exhibits in the roadside attraction are specimens they collected and left behind for some reason. But I'm getting ahead of myself."

He looked at the floor for a moment before speaking again. "They gave me a job as a sort of handyman— exactly the kind of job I'd been looking for. Just doing physical work was restful after what I'd been through

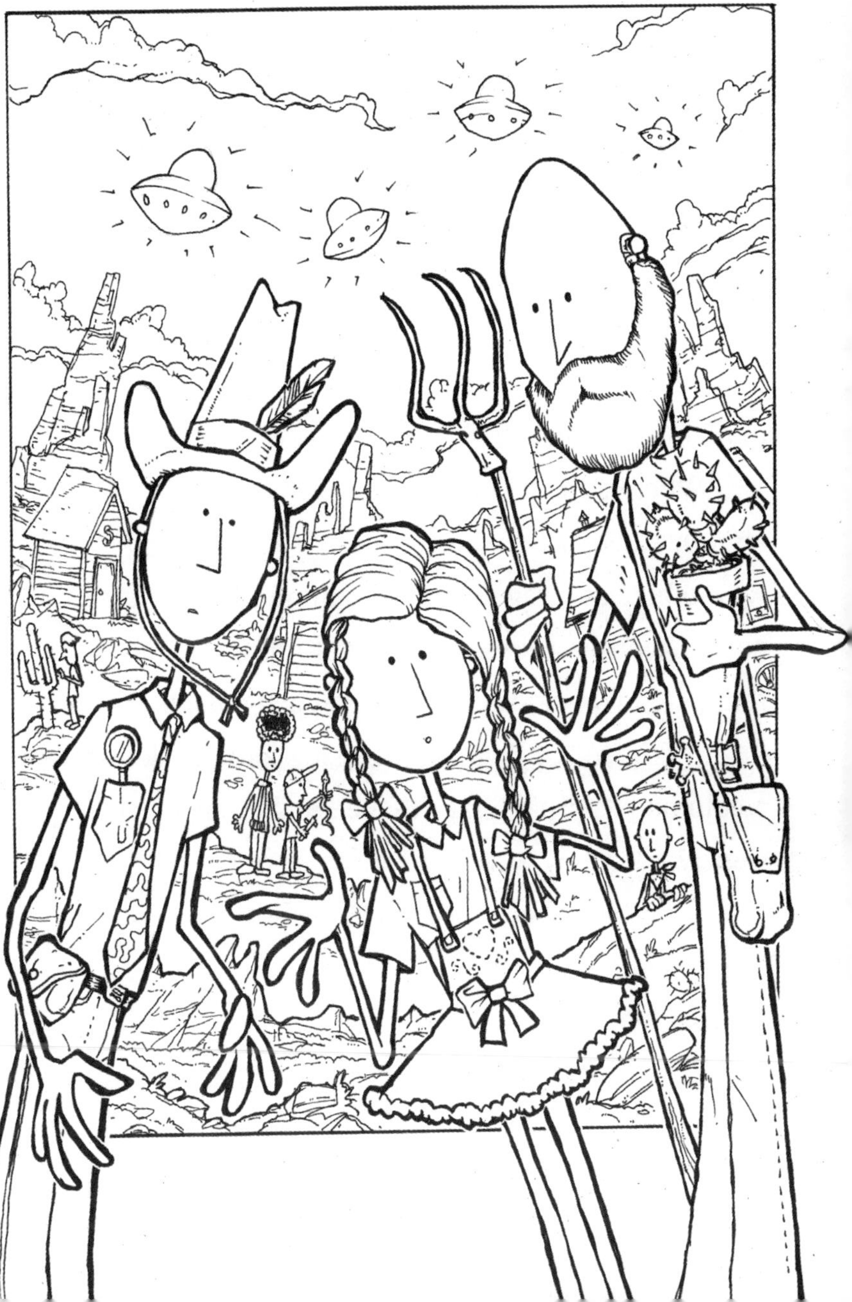

in the big city. I did everything—cooking, cleaning, painting, the works. The only problem was that they wouldn't let me go in this garage. When I asked any of them what was inside, they only smiled.

"After a few weeks I asked Cordic—the fellow who seemed to be in charge—if he and his friends were aliens, and he said yes. In fact, they had collected more than enough specimens and were about to return to their home planet."

"Where's that?" I asked.

"Out there somewhere," Mr. Moppit said as he waved his hand vaguely at the ceiling. "They were never specific. Anyway, one night I heard a loud roaring and a whoosh. When I stepped outside, I was just in time to see their saucer rising into the sky on a column of purple light. It faded and disappeared shortly after they were gone."

"Your big chance to see what was in the garage!" Rocky exclaimed.

"Right. I ran here immediately. Before I could get in, I actually had to break off the lock. When I got the door open at last, I found this interociter thingy.

Tinkering with it has become a bit of a hobby."

"Is it safe to mess with?" Rocky asked. He had recently had a bad experience while taking apart an electric clock.

"So far," Mr. Moppit said.

I hopped down from my stool and took a closer look at the interociter. I even touched it. It was solid, but the surface was warm, not cold as I had expected. We heard a footstep on the gravel outside. Rocky and I looked at each other, eyes wide with fear. "Mom and Dad!" he cried.

As things turned out, I wish it had been Mom and Dad.

A creature entered the garage and gaped at us, its mouth opening and closing like a fish's. It looked like a rhinoceros, only instead of four strong, stumpy legs, this creature walked on hundreds of slender tentacles. One of its front tentacles was holding some kind of machine.

"I want the spider in slime," it demanded in a gruff voice, "and I want it now." It waved the machine in our direction. I was taking bets that the thing was a weapon.

MASHY NEBLICK

This new guy was really scary. I realized now that Mr. Moppit was just strange. But this guy seemed determined to hurt us if he didn't get what he wanted.

"Spider in slime?" Mr. Moppit asked, his voice shaking. He looked as frightened as Rocky and I were. He glanced down at the big wrench he'd dropped earlier.

The rhinoceros creature gave a cry, and kicked the wrench aside with a tentacle. "Give it now!" he demanded, and aimed his weapon at Mr. Moppit.

"I have no idea what you're talking about," Mr. Moppit said.

"I am Mashy Neblick," the rhino creature said. "Do not attempt to defy me!"

"It wouldn't occur to me to defy you," Mr. Moppit said reasonably. "Perhaps if you could describe this spider in slime, we could help you look for it."

Mashy Neblick thought that over as if he was actually considering Mr. Moppit's offer. "It is a hairy spider embedded in a round dish of amber slime. Last I heard, the Toubij had it."

"Yes!" Mr. Moppit cried. "The Toubij! The're the ones who lived here before, the aliens who gave me the roadside attraction and the motor hotel!"

"Aha!" Mashy Neblick cried. "Take me to them!"

"They've all gone home, I'm afraid," Mr. Moppit said, as if he were really sorry. "Back to their home planet."

"Did they take it with them?"

Mr. Moppit seemed astonished by the question. "I don't know," he said. "Until you came along, I had no idea such a thing existed." He nodded as if agreeing with himself. "It may still be here, but the Toubij may have hidden it to keep it away from you, Mr. Mashy Neblick."

Bold talk, I thought. I was impressed with Mr.

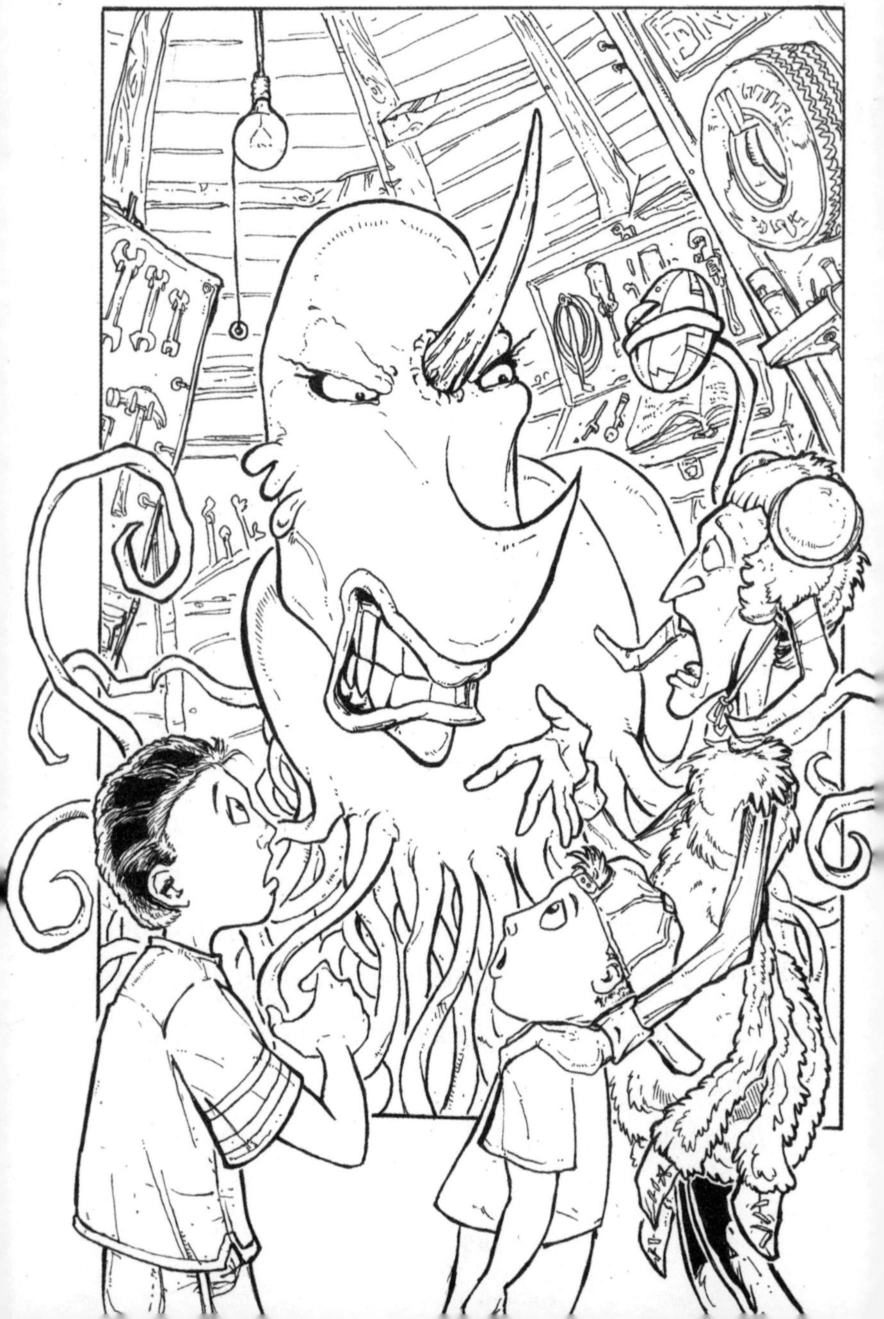

Moppit's courage.

"You will help me find it," Mashy Neblick shouted. He leaned forward and took a closer look at the interociter. "What is that?" he asked, as he gestured with a tentacle.

"I call it an interociter."

"Primitive," Mashy Neblick commented.

"Maybe. I don't know what it does. Do you?"

"Hmph. You don't know much."

"I know good from evil," Mr. Moppit replied.

Mashy Neblick looked through the hole in the side of the interociter.

"No spider in slime in there," Mr. Moppit assured him. "I've been working on the interociter for months, and I haven't seen it."

Mashy Neblick nodded. "You will help me find it now!" he shouted. He motioned with his weapon. We walked out of the garage with him herding us along.

The night suddenly seemed darker and colder than it had been. The stars were too far away to help. The desert might as well have been the surface of the Moon. I wished Mom and Dad were there, though I didn't know what they could do against Mashy Neblick and his weapon. If Mashy Neblick disintegrated the three of us, Mom and Dad might think that Mr. Moppit had abducted us. For some reason, what the parents might think bothered me more than the actual disintegration.

"Where are we going?" I asked as we walked.

"Silence!" Mashy Neblick shouted.

Rocky's face was all scrunched up. I could see he was thinking hard. "But," he said, "if the spider in slime is so dangerous in the wrong hands, why did the Toubij hide it? Why not just destroy it?"

"Because," Mashy Neblick cried, "it is too valuable and useful! Even the Toubij knew that!"

"So, Mr. Neblick," I asked carefully, "what exactly does the spider in slime do?"

"Its bite will give me superpowers."

"Like leaping over tall buildings in a single bound?" Rocky asked. "Bouncing bullets off your chest? Bending steel in your bare hands?"

"All that and more," Mashy Neblick assured him.

"Cool," Rocky said.

I didn't think it was so cool. Mashy Neblick was the last guy I'd want to see with superpowers. Chances were pretty good he wouldn't be fighting for "truth, justice, and the American way." But I kept my opinion to myself.

No one said anything more while Mashy Neblick marched us down the long side of the motel. I wondered whether I should wake up Mom and Dad if I had the chance, or if that would only get them into trouble, too.

"We will search all rooms," Mashy Neblick began. "We will start…" He was no longer watching us, or even the motel building. He was staring at our car.

"What is that. Thing. Over. There?" he asked, and pointed with a delicate tentacle. He seemed very excited.

"It's a car," I said. "An automobile. Four rubber tires. Internal-combustion engine. Automatic transmission. Sometimes air conditioning. Right now it doesn't work very well."

Mashy Neblick's mouth was opening and closing really fast as he walked toward the car. He *really* looked like a fish now. Rocky and Mr. Moppit were going to follow him, but I held them back.

"I have heard of such things," Mashy Neblick said. "But I never imagined I would be so fortunate as to see one. Show me this internal-combustion engine." I showed him how to open the hood. When it was up, he stared at the engine as if it were the most interesting thing he'd ever seen. From a pocket he pulled out a silver egg.

I sidled away from the car until I was standing with Rocky and Mr. Moppit. We watched for a moment while Mashy Neblick aimed the small end of the silver egg at the engine. The end grew into a long narrow stick, which he stuck down among the wires and hoses and belts.

I motioned Rocky and Mr. Moppit toward the office, and without a word we quietly moved closer to it.

"Hey," Mashy Neblick called, as he turned and spotted us.

No point in sneaking now. We ran for the office door with Mashy Neblick gaining on us.

CHAPTER EIGHT

We ran into the office and slammed the door.

"We can't stay here long," Mr. Moppit said. "That silver egg is a nanowrench, an alien tool made of millions of microscopic independent bits. It can analyze and fix any mechanical problem. I never actually used one myself. The bits can attach themselves together in any way, allowing the nanowrench to take the form of any tool"—he was interrupted by a loud whine and a terrible grinding noise against the door—"like a power saw, for instance. Come on!"

He ran for the back of the room and quickly raised the window. He climbed out with Rocky right behind him. I just made it out the window myself before something on the other side of the door punched in a big uneven circle of wood. Mashy Neblick looked in through the hole.

"Those who defy me are always sorry," he cried, and crawled in through the hole, tentacle over tentacle.

"He'll be here in a second," Mr. Moppit said as we huddled against the wall of the building. "What should we do?"

"Find the spider in slime," I said. "Maybe we can use it against him."

"Right," Mr. Moppit said, and hurried us along to the next window down. It was the bathroom window of room number one. He tore off the screen and threw open the window. After all three of us were inside, he closed the window and locked it.

I turned around and was surprised to see that we weren't in one of the Spider Motel rooms. We seemed to be inside an enormous mechanical clock. Gears and levers and springs went on for miles and rose far above our heads—each grinding along in a deliberate, purposeful way. A loud ticking sounded every second or so. It may not have been a clock at all, but it sure looked like one.

"Where are we?" I asked, aware that Mashy Neblick would be on top of us in a moment.

"The Spider isn't just a motel," Mr. Moppit explained while he looked behind me with some fear. "Some rooms are normal, like the ones I rented to you and your parents, but others are really portals to other worlds."

"That's why you were so careful about which rooms you gave us," Rocky said. "You didn't want us to get lost in another world."

"Right," Mr. Moppit said. "If you walked into the wrong one, you might never be seen again."

Rocky glanced around fearfully.

I didn't blame him for being worried. "Is the spider in slime in here?" I asked. The place was huge. It would take hours, maybe days, to search through it all.

"That's just it. I don't know for sure. I just wanted to get away from Mashy Neblick so we'd have time to think."

We heard a bump, then a thump, then a scratching noise.

"There, see it?" Mr. Moppit said, speaking hurriedly. "Floating in the air there. You can just see the outline of the window we came in by. And at the other end of the room, there's the door through which we'll leave."

The door and window to which he pointed were no more than ghosts of themselves. We walked to the door—it was only a few steps away, no farther than it would have been in the motel room—and walked out into the normal desert night. Before the door shut behind us, I heard Mashy Neblick threatening us.

"Well, I'm relieved," I said.

"Come on," Mr. Moppit said. "We haven't lost him yet."

Rocky and I followed him to the next door down.

"Master key," Mr. Moppit said as he rattled the key in the lock.

"Good thing Mashy Neblick doesn't have one," Rocky said while we waited impatiently for Mr.

Moppit to open the door.

"He doesn't need one. He has that nanowrench," Mr. Moppit said. He flung open the door, and ushered us into the room beyond.

Suddenly it was daytime. At first the heat felt really good, but that didn't last long. Soon I was sweating like mad. Two pastel suns, a blue one and a green one, were bright in the sky. I felt heavier than I usually did.

"I can hardly move," Rocky said.

"Take it slow," Mr. Moppit said. "We won't be here long."

Sure enough, I could see the ghost of the bathroom window hanging in the air nearby.

"What's that?" Rocky asked, and pointed down a long incline of sand dunes. In the valley at the bottom was a city of white stone. Some of the structures had toppled over, and they looked as if they'd been built from giant sugar cubes. But the shapes of the buildings were nothing humans had ever thought of. I couldn't begin to describe them.

"Abandoned city," Mr. Moppit said.

"I want to explore," Rocky exclaimed.

"We don't have time," I said.

"Besides," Mr. Moppit continued for me, "if we were to run around down there for a few hours, we might never find this spot again. We'd be stuck on this planet." He opened the ghost bathroom window and urged us to climb through it. We did so, and a moment later he climbed through after us.

Once again we were back on Earth. I heard Mashy Neblick shouting in the room behind us, wherever the insides really were.

The next room contained a hot, steamy jungle full of autumn colors.

"Not a dry heat," I said to Rocky, hoping the little joke would relieve some of the tension I was feeling. It didn't.

Rocky just nodded. I was as tense as ever.

We were standing at the end of a path that led around the individual roots of trees that rose into the clouds. Each root itself was actually the size of a tree. The trunks of the trees were as big around as office buildings. The ground was littered with club-size sticks, twigs from these enormous trees. Somebody nearby shrieked on our left. Answering shrieks came from our right.

"We're surrounded," I said. I was terrified.

Mr. Moppit looked around, his eyes wide. If he had any ideas, he wasn't sharing them with Rocky and me.

"Aha!" Mashy Neblick cried.

We turned and saw the alien slither through a hole in the ghost window. No problem, I thought. The door through which we would exit couldn't be far away.

"Come on, guys," I said, and took up the lead.

Suddenly something leaped onto the path in front of me. It was lobstery, but man-size. It shrieked at us, and its mouthparts clicked as it worked them. I froze.

"Where is the spider in slime?" Mashy Neblick cried from behind us. "Tell me, and I will allow you to escape!"

"We don't know," Mr. Moppit cried back at him.

With one motion I bent down, grabbed one of those club-size twigs, and flung it at Mashy Neblick. It spun through the air and hit him on one tentacle. He screamed and ran toward me, lopsided because of the pain. I grabbed him by a handy tentacle and swung him into the big lobster guy. They went down in a pile, tangled up together.

"Come on," I cried, and ran for the ghost door without looking back. I climbed out and was back in the familiar desert night. A moment later Rocky and Mr. Moppit stood near me, breathing hard.

"That bought us a few minutes," Mr. Moppit said. He quickly opened the next door down and went in. Rocky and I followed.

I almost lost my dinner.

We were standing on a ghost floor in the middle of zillions and zillions of cubic light-years of empty space. I could still breathe, and I wasn't colder than I had been before, but the place looked cold. I couldn't keep myself from shivering.

"Shouldn't we be suffocating and exploding?" Rocky asked.

"No, no. Each of us is surrounded by a protective bubble. We have been right from the beginning. It's only out here in interstellar space that you can see it."

Mr. Moppit was right. I could see what looked like ghost eggs around him and Rocky. I held up my hands

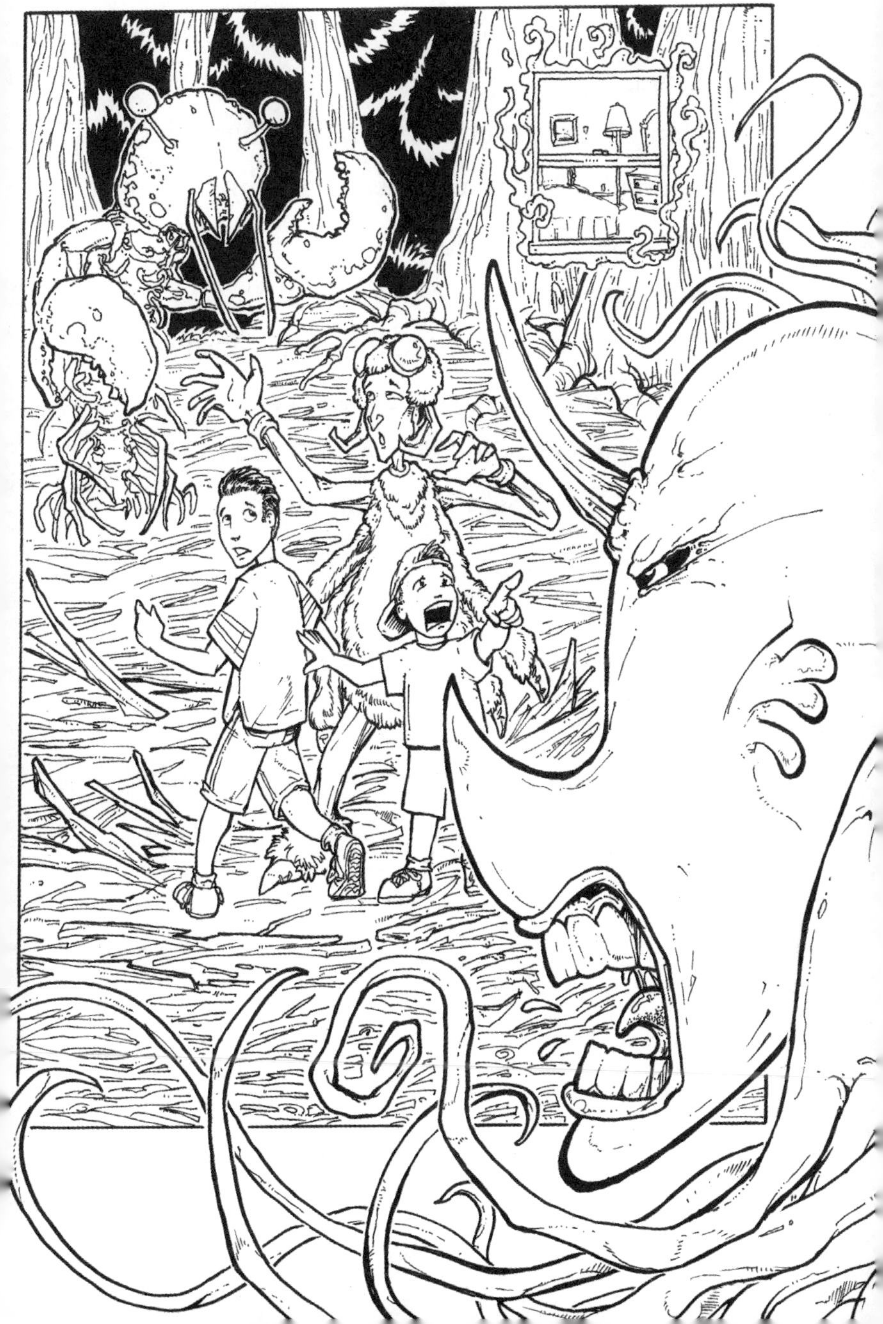

and could see my own bubble. "No spider in slime here," I said.

Suddenly Mashy Neblick burst in through the ghost door. He grabbed the nearest person to him, who was Rocky, and held him close.

Rocky yelped.

"If you ever want to see him again," Mashy Neblick threatened, "give me the spider!"

Mr. Moppit and I didn't have a chance to move before he dragged Rocky back out the door.

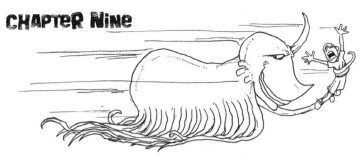

CHAPTER Nine

HiDe iN PLAiN SiGHT

Interstellar space was suddenly a lot emptier than it had been a moment before. I rushed after Rocky and Mashy Neblick. When I got outside, nobody was there. I looked up and down the cement sidewalk along the side of the motel building while I vibrated with fear and anger. I didn't even know in which direction Mashy Neblick had taken Rocky. I had to do something, but I didn't know what. Mr. Moppit came out of the room and joined me.

"Where did they go?" he asked.

"You're the mind reader! You tell me." I didn't usually use that tone on adults, but I was feeling pretty bad about losing my brother.

"Mind reader?" Mr. Moppit asked, confused.

"You knew what we wanted for dinner," I

exclaimed. "Can't you read Mashy Neblick's mind?"

"No, no, no!" Mr. Moppit said, with despair in his voice. "When it comes to food, I have a sort of feeling, an intuition. I can't read minds any more than you can."

"Then we have to find that spider in slime."

"Why? To trade for your brother? Not a bad idea."

"I don't want to bargain with Mashy Neblick. I want to beat him. He told us that the bite of the spider would give a person superpowers. I want to become super so I can save Rocky."

"I can see how strongly you feel about that," Mr. Moppit said. "But I really don't know where the spider is."

Feeling lost and alone, I looked out at the desert. I didn't like to think about what Mashy Neblick might be doing to Rocky, or what my parents would do to me for losing him. "Listen," I said. "In school, my teacher read us a story by Edgar Allan Poe called 'The Purloined Letter.' It's about somebody who steals a letter and nobody can find it because he hides it where nobody would think to look—in plain sight. I bet the spider in slime is somewhere around here in plain sight. Where would you not notice a spider in slime?"

Mr. Moppit thought for a moment. He smiled. "The roadside attraction," he exclaimed.

"That's what I was thinking!"

As we hurried to the roadside attraction, I expected Mashy Neblick and Rocky to pop up any moment—or maybe that was wishful thinking.

"If we find the spider—" Mr. Moppit began as he jogged beside me.

"When we find—" I interrupted him.

"When we find the spider, I want to be the one to take the bite. After all, we don't really know what the bite will do to a person. We have only Mashy Neblick's word. And it's bound to be worse for a kid than for an adult."

"I want to save my brother," I protested.

"What does it matter who saves him, as long as he gets saved?" Mr. Moppit pointed out.

I could see the logic in what he was saying. "All right," I said, relieved. "Thanks." Sometimes it's nice to have grown-ups around.

We passed the Spider Café and came to the roadside attraction. Mr. Moppit unlocked the building and flicked on the lights. He started searching at one side of the room, and I started at the other.

I went down one row of display cases and up another, stopping to inspect each exhibit, making sure it was not a spider in slime disguised in some way. I saw a lot of funny-shaped rocks, mutant cacti, odd photos, rusty weapons, and a genuine gold nugget.

A card written in sort-of-English stood in front of each exhibit. One of them said, COULD BE CACTUS OF MANY INTERESTING FACE. Another said, FINE INCIDENT OF METAL THING. My favorite was, BIG LAUGHS INSIDE! Other cards made even less sense. Not one exhibit held any promise. Of course, a lot of them were missing, with only a WE'LL BE BACK SOON! card in its place.

I slumped against the wall and waited for Mr. Moppit to finish. I was feeling more depressed than angry now. I would never see my rotten little brother again, and it was all my fault. How would I live with myself? And to make matters worse, my parents would

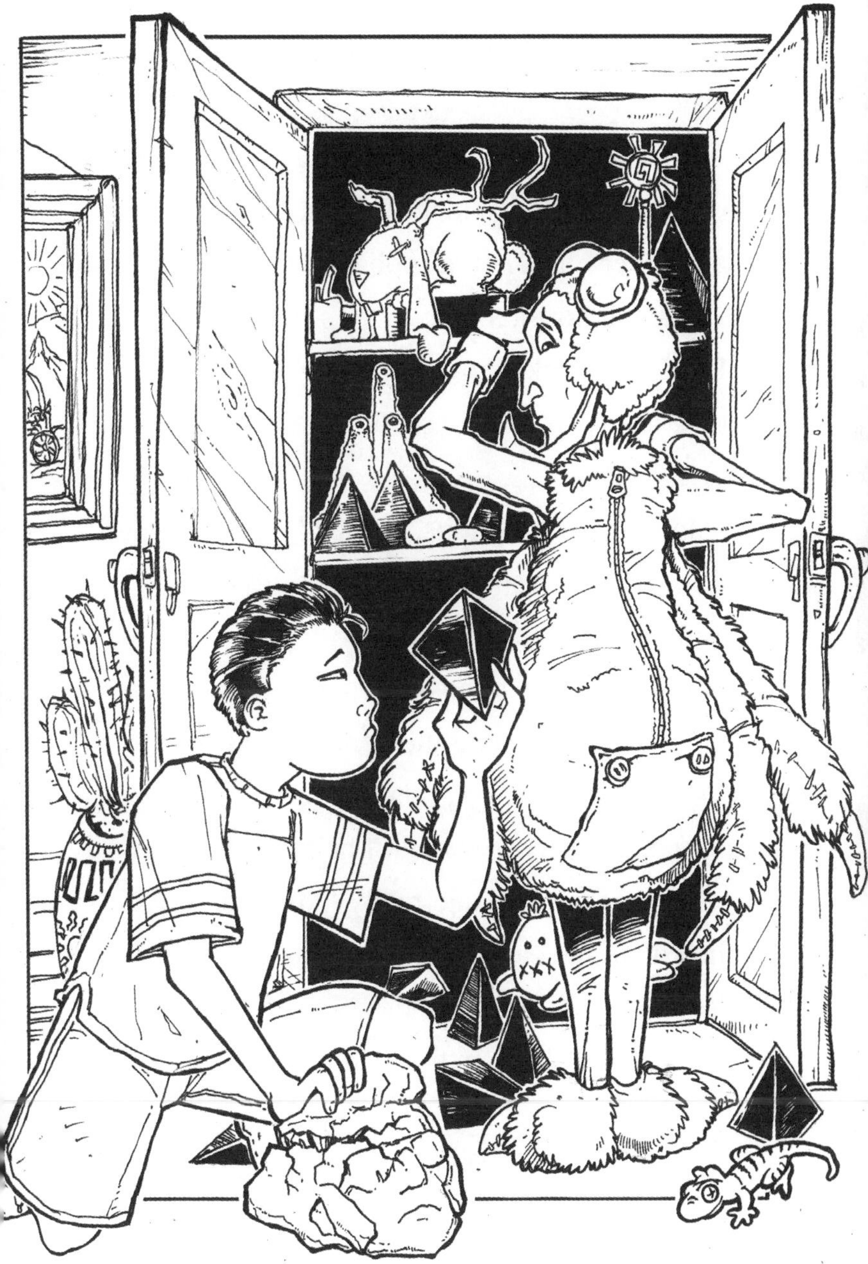

probably not believe me when I told them how it happened.

Really, Mom and Dad, Rocky was abducted by an alien looking for a spider in slime. Oh, sure. That would go over big. They'd probably put me into some kind of mental hospital.

Mr. Moppit looked pretty glum when he joined me at the door. "Well?" I asked, although I knew the answer.

"Many amazing exhibits," he said, "but nothing I would describe as a spider in slime. You?"

"Nada. Zip. Zilch. Bupkis."

For a while we just looked around the room. I wanted to cry—if ever a moment seemed worth shedding a few tears over, this was it—but I had work to do, and crying wouldn't help. Then I stopped just staring at the room and really looked at it. We'd searched in all the cases, but there was one place we hadn't looked.

"What do you keep in that cabinet in the corner of the room?" I asked.

"Just the broken exhibits," Mr. Moppit said.

"Let's go look," I said, and ran to the cabinet. It was locked! I pounded on the door and kicked it until Mr. Moppit finally got there and unlocked it.

"Sorry," I said. "But I'm feeling a little frustrated right now."

"Hmm. Guilty, too, I bet," Mr. Moppit suggested.

I nodded. If I hadn't awakened Rocky, he wouldn't be gone now.

"Each of us makes his own decisions," Mr. Moppit told me. "Rocky didn't have to go with you."

"I guess." I was not convinced. I pulled open the cabinet. Just as Mr. Moppit said, inside were broken exhibits—a cracked rock that may have looked like Elvis at one time, a petrified jackalope with limbs missing, an average-looking rock whose card said, WILL FLOAT WHEN MARTIANS NEAR. No spiders of any description.

"What's this?" I asked, and picked up a small black pyramid. A dozen or so of them were scattered across the cabinet shelves. They definitely did not fit in with the rest of the objects in the cabinet.

CHAPTER TEN

BLACK PYRAMIDS

I held up one of the black pyramids. It weighed about the same as a baseball. The five sides were smooth and so shiny I could see my face in them.

Mr. Moppit shrugged. "I don't know what they are," he said. "The Toubij left a lot of them lying around the roadside attraction. I figured they were of interest only to the aliens, so I put them away with the broken stuff."

"Hmm," I said. I rooted around inside the cabinet, pulled out all the black pyramids, and set them up in a row on top of the nearest display case.

Mr. Moppit bent down to study them. "They all look exactly the same," he said.

"Did they go with these?" I asked, and pulled

out a stack of cards. The top one said, COULD BE A MOUNTEBANK IF SO. The next one said, A GOOD COLOR FOR THREE FEET.

Mr. Moppit looked over my shoulder at the cards. "These don't make any more sense than the others," he said. "Look at this: A FISH WHEN IT SPINS."

"Still," I said, "we've looked at every other exhibit. It's gotta be here!" I hefted up one of the pyramids and picked at one edge. That seemed useless, so I stopped.

"Maybe the spider isn't here at all," Mr. Moppit said. "The Toubij might've hidden it in the Spider Café. Or they could have taken it with them when they left."

While I racked my brain for places where the Toubij might have hidden the spider, I casually stood the pyramid on its point and spun it like a top. Mr. Moppit and I watched it. Just before it fell over, something began to happen.

"It was going to open," Mr. Moppit said excitedly.

I spun the pyramid again, harder this time.

This time we could see that the pyramid wasn't opening. It was changing, morphing into something else. By the time it had stopped spinning, it was something like a clear glass pine cone with spiny things sticking out of it.

"Alien plant?" I suggested.

"I don't know," Mr. Moppit said. "Try another one."

"Yeah," I said, with growing excitement. "Maybe the spider is one of these."

I spun another pyramid, and it made a small red egg with a hole on the big end and a green button on the other. We didn't know what it was—musical instrument? TV remote control? thought projector?— but we knew it wasn't a spider in slime. Mr. Moppit and I each spun pyramids. I'd spun five before Mr. Moppit whistled softly.

"It's here," he said.

My latest pyramid had just become what looked like a pile of straw. Straw? I looked over at what Mr. Moppit had found.

It was a flat dish a little bigger around than my fist. Floating inside some orange stuff—the slime, I assumed—was a big spider.

"A tarantula," Mr. Moppit said.

"Right. Which card do you think goes with it?"

We looked through all the cards. Two seemed like possibilities. One said EIGHT HANDS, WARM HEART. The other said, NOT A TRUE BUG BUTT.

"I don't get it," Mr. Moppit said.

"Maybe there's nothing to get. Come on, let's open the dish. We have to save Rocky."

"Right." Mr. Moppit picked up the dish. Holding it in one hand, he tried to twist off the top with the other. "It's tight," he said.

"Try again."

Mr. Moppit picked up the dish and closed his eyes. As he tried to pull the two halves of the dish apart, beads of sweat broke out on his forehead. "Ah," he said at last, and the two halves of the dish came away from each other. Mr. Moppit set the bottom of the dish on a display case. He and I studied it.

"Go ahead," I said.

Gingerly, as if he were picking up something small and fragile (which is exactly what he was in fact, doing), he lifted the tarantula by one leg. As soon as it

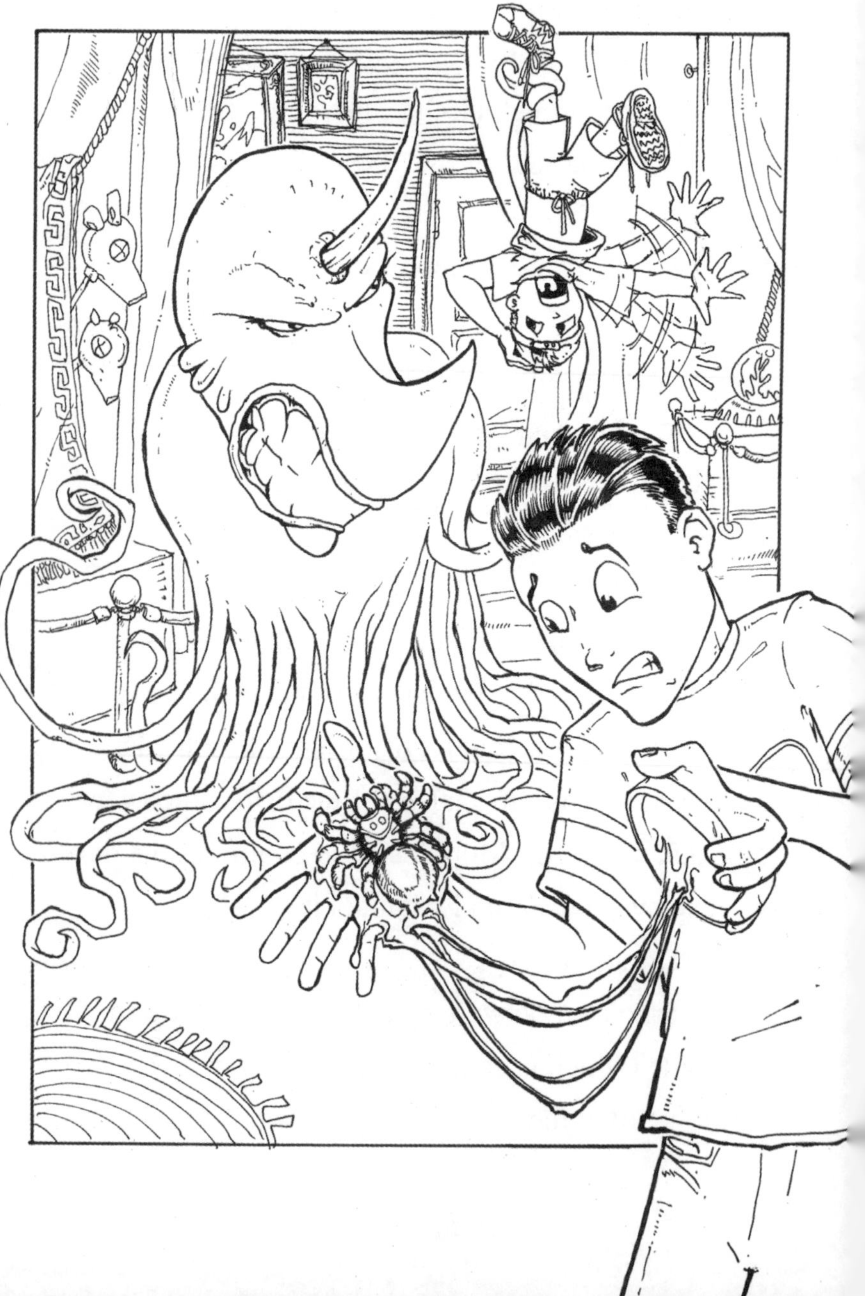

was out of the slime it began to wriggle.

"Give me the spider," shouted a now-familiar voice, "or your companion will die horribly."

We were both startled by the arrival of Mashy Neblick, who was gripping Rocky by the leg. My brother looked terrified.

While Mr. Moppit was distracted by Mashy Neblick's arrival, the spider took the opportunity to wriggle free of Mr. Moppit's grip. It dropped onto my arm. As I looked at it in horror, it bit me!

CHAPTER ELEVEN

ARACHNOR

My heart thudded loudly in my chest, and I broke into a cold sweat. I shook the spider onto the floor, where it skittered under one of the display cases as my arm bulged and reddened. I was sure now that Mashy Neblick had lied about the result of the spider bite. I wouldn't become a superhero. I was going to die.

But I didn't die—though at first I wanted to. My body felt as if it were full of bees, all zooming around and buzzing and stinging. The way a tub fills with water, my head was filling with pictures and ideas I'd never had before. And I watched with horrified fascination as my body swelled up like a balloon. Buds sprouted on my sides, and they grew into long appendages—arms? legs?—that soon were covered with thick black hair. My clothes became tighter, and instead of running shoes I was now wearing green boots that came up to my knees. I was growing taller, too.

The whole process took less than a minute. When it was over, I was taller than Mr. Moppit and had the body of Arnold Schwarzenegger on a good day. I wore a blue form-fitting uniform with a green spider web on my chest. My hands were green, too, and I had complete control over my extra appendages. All in all, I was one cool dude. Mashy Neblick looked as astonished as Mr. Moppit and Rocky did.

"I am Arachnor!" I intoned with a voice deeper and more mature than Darth Vader's. "Let the boy go now!"

"Of course," Mashy Neblick said. He suddenly pushed Rocky at me and dived for the floor beneath the display case where the spider was hiding.

"Take Rocky, Mr. Moppit," I said, and reached down for Mashy Neblick. I pulled him to his feet—er, tentacles—but, using an alien karate move, he twisted away.

"You have your child," Mashy Neblick whined.

"Allow me to take the spider and go."

"And allow you to loot, pillage, and otherwise despoil the universe?" I asked sarcastically. "I laugh up my web at you." My laugh boomed through the room.

"In that case," Mashy Neblick said, as if he were thinking over his options, "I'll just go." Moving swiftly on his tentacles, he bolted for the door.

I fell onto my eight legs and ran toward the door, moving faster than I thought possible. When I got outside I didn't see Mashy Neblick. I was sure that his plan was to make me pursue him, and while I was doing so he would come back and find the spider. But I, Arachnor, had a plan of my own!

I quickly spun a thick net of supersilk over the door. Only a matter/antimatter weapon or my own spider spit would be able to get through it. Then, still on all eights, I searched for Mashy Neblick.

I picked up his scent through the soles of my boots, which is the way spiders smell, I guess. His odor made him fairly easy to follow. But he moved as fast as I did myself, so he was always a little ahead of me. Suddenly, red beams of energy buzzed around me, kicking up sand as they struck the ground. One nicked me in the leg. It hurt, but I kept moving. Arachnor does not give up so easily!

I looked up and saw Mashy Neblick on the roof of the motel building, silhouetted by the stars. While he took aim at me, I sprang onto the roof and knocked the weapon from his tentacle. "Make it easy on yourself, Mashy Neblick," I said. "Surrender now." For some reason I was not bothered by the fact that I wouldn't know what to do with him if I caught him.

Infuriated, Mashy Neblick growled and rushed at me. He nearly knocked me off the roof. We grappled. He and I were about evenly matched, so for a while we just rocked up and back. Then Mashy Neblick pushed me over, and we rolled across the roof of the motel. We came to the edge and fell over. Instinctively I attached a lifeline of supersilk to the eave and reeled it out as Mashy Neblick and I fell. I stopped just short of the ground, but Mashy Neblick kept going. He struck the dirt—hard.

He was up immediately and pounding at me as if I were a punching bag. The punches didn't hurt, exactly, but they weren't pleasant either. I swung back and forth wildly on my lifeline. At the right moment, I let go of the supersilk and leaped onto Mashy Neblick.

As we struggled across the parking lot, first I got the upper hand and then he did. He threw sand into my face, which blinded me for a moment. In that instant, his tentacles wrapped around my throat. Unable to see, I flailed at him. We fell to the ground as more tentacles wrapped around my head. I took a chance and bit him on the nearest tentacle.

He screamed and immediately let go. But by that time it was too late. He was already slowing down. I quickly lassoed him with supersilk and pulled him toward me. He couldn't even protest. When I had him within arm's length, I plucked his nanowrench from his pocket. By now he'd stopped moving altogether. I hefted him over my shoulder and carried him back to the roadside attraction.

I spit onto the supersilk over the door, and it fell away like tissue paper in the rain. I used it to wrap him up in a cocoon of supersilk, for good measure. Then I carried Mashy Neblick inside and dropped him on the

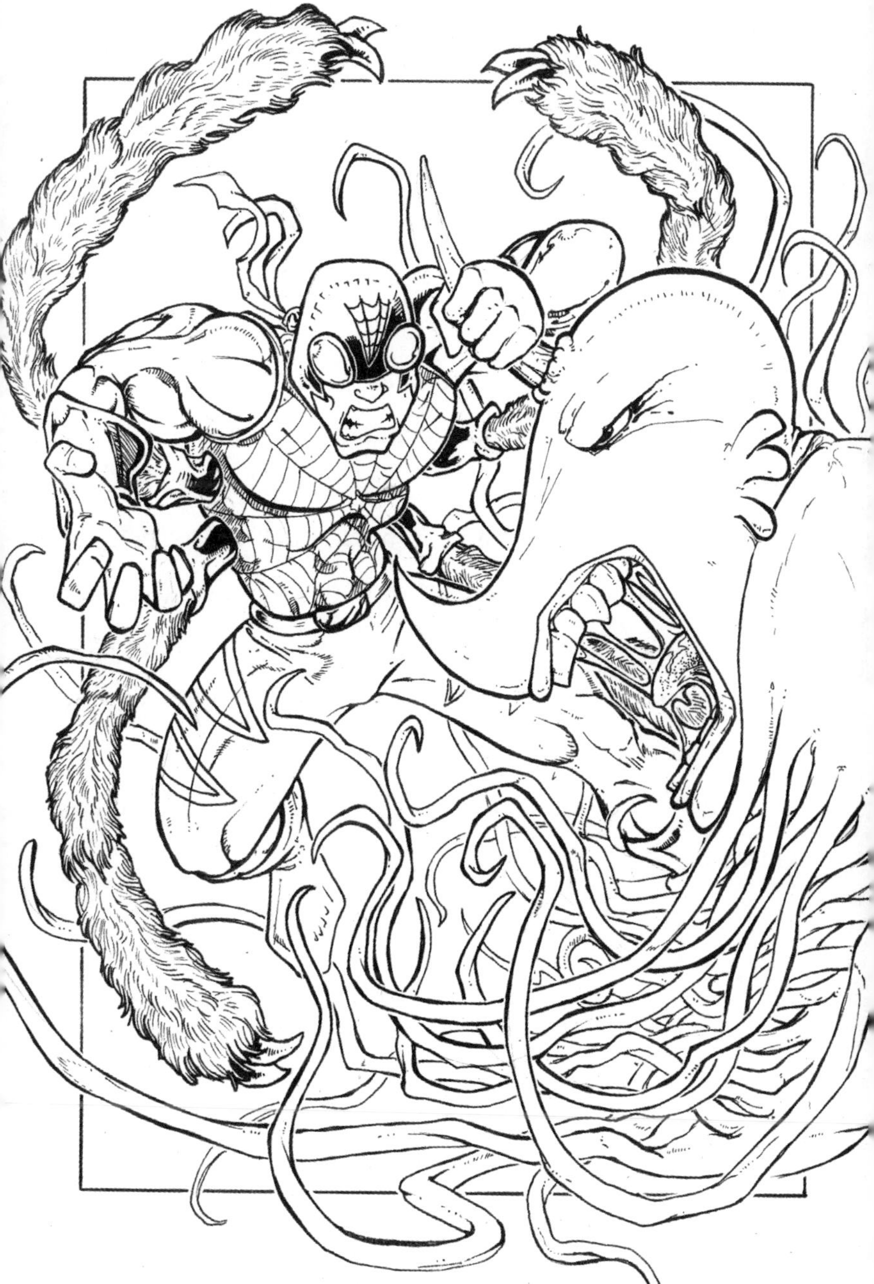

floor in front of Rocky and Mr. Moppit.

"Is he dead?" Rocky asked.

"Not dead," I assured him. "Just asleep. The supersilk cocoon will keep him that way."

"Wow," Rocky said. "Having a superhero for a brother is way cool."

"Thanks, Rocky," I said, and mussed his hair.

"We still need to find the spider," Mr. Moppit reminded me.

I nodded and made a keening sound. A few seconds later the spider peered out from under the display case, then it emerged. I gently picked up the spider and put it back into its slime case. The case had been resting on the countertop all this time.

"That about wraps that up," said Mr. Moppit with a chuckle.

CHAPTER TWELVE

ON THE ROAD AGAIN

"**H**ow are you feeling, Rocky?" I asked, in my booming hero's voice.

"My leg's a little sore where he grabbed me, but I'm okay."

"Brave lad," I said. I never would have said such a thing if I were just his brother. But I was still Arachnor and could get away with talking like that. I could have sung, "Here I come to save the day," but it seemed a little late for that.

"What are we going to do with him?" Rocky asked, and used one foot to prod the cocoon that contained Mashy Neblick.

"Oh, I have some ideas," Mr. Moppit said. He

dragged the cocoon into a corner and leaned it against the wall.

"Very well, then, I leave it to you. Meanwhile, I have another job to do. Come along," I said to Rocky. "You can watch."

I went outside and opened the hood of the family car. After studying the engine for a few seconds, I pointed the small end of the nanowrench at it. Blue lightning crackled from the nanowrench and fell all over the engine like hundreds of hands, seemingly testing where it hurt and making it all better. After a few moments, the lightning stopped. Suddenly everything was quiet.

"Did you fix it?" Rocky asked.

"Of course," I said. I tossed the nanowrench to Mr. Moppit. "You keep it," I said. "You'll probably figure out how to run it yourself, eventually. When you do, maybe you'll be able to repair the interociter with it."

"Hey, thanks," Mr. Moppit said as he turned the tool over and over in his hands. He seemed genuinely pleased. "And you can have this." He handed me the spider in its slime case. "Just a little something to remember me by."

Rocky laughed. "I don't think we're going to forget you or Mashy Neblick any time soon." He took a long, hard look at me. "Aren't you shorter than you were?"

I looked down at myself. "You're right," I exclaimed. My muscles had wilted too. They seemed to be getting smaller as I watched. My skintight outfit was also getting looser. "What's going on?" I asked. My voice squeaked.

"The spider bite is wearing off," Mr. Moppit said. "By morning you should be yourself again."

"Oh, my gosh, morning," I said, squeaking again.

"Yes," Mr. Moppit said "You've been up most of the night. I'd advise you to get some rest. You will probably be moving on tomorrow."

It wasn't until Mr. Moppit mentioned that we'd been up all night that I noticed how tired I felt. Now both Rocky and I stretched. "Sounds good to me," Rocky said through a yawn.

Mr. Moppit walked us back to room seven. I heard snoring coming from room eight. Apparently, nothing had disturbed our parents' rest.

"Good night, boys," Mr. Moppit said. "See you at breakfast."

We wished him good night. I unlocked the door, and we went into our room. Rocky shucked his clothes and climbed into bed immediately. But I was still changing. I felt funny—a little dizzy, and as if my entire body were vibrating. Things that Arachnor knew were fading from my memory. I sat down in the one armchair in the room and waited until I felt more like myself.

I awoke the next morning with golden desert sunlight pouring in through the windows. I knew I was myself again by the way I fit into the chair. Not only was I smaller than Arachnor, but the extra legs were gone. I also had no idea how to do a lot of things, including how to spin supersilk or how to use a nanowrench. There were some things about being Arachnor that I would miss.

Rocky was gone. For a moment I thought Mashy Neblick had taken him again, but then it occurred to me that Rocky was probably next door with the parents. I sat for a while and enjoyed being a familiar shape and size.

I felt a big lump in my jacket pocket. It turned out to be the spider in its slime case. So that part of the adventure had really happened. Would the spider begin to move if I took it out of the slime? If it bit me, would I become Arachnor again? I wanted to know the answers to these questions, but not right now. Right now I just wanted to be me.

When the novelty of just being myself again wore off, I went outside. The land spread out before me like a model of the desert. The air was pleasantly warm instead of the blast furnace it would be not very much later. I went next door and found Mom and Rocky sitting on the bed while Dad stood in front of the mirror buttoning his shirt.

"We slept like a couple of rocks," Mom said, sounding pretty chipper. "How about you?"

I glanced at Rocky, trying to see how much, if anything, he'd told our parents about the events of last night.

"Exactly like a rock," I said. Actually, I was pretty tired. Just walking around felt like a lot of work.

Mom accepted that statement, so I guessed that Rocky had kept his mouth shut for once.

"Who's for breakfast?" Dad asked. "Can't fix the car on an empty stomach."

I just nodded. I remembered using the nanowrench on the car the night before, but I didn't actually know whether I had fixed it or not.

We walked along the side of the building until we came to room three. A big, ragged hole had been punched through the door.

"Yeow!" Dad exclaimed. "This door didn't have a hole in it last night." He stooped to look in through the hole. Would he see the clock? the desert? the forest? outer space? Whatever it was, I knew the jig was up. Rocky and I shared a worried glance, and I held my breath.

"I don't know of any animal that can do that," Mom said.

"Elephant?" Rocky suggested. "Buffalo?"

"We're just lucky whatever-it-was didn't break into our rooms," Dad said, straightening. He made no comment about the room inside.

"If we can start the car," Mom said, "then we're lucky.

"I have complete confidence," Dad said, and walked on.

As we passed the door both Rocky and I looked in through the hole. Inside was just a motel room very much like the other ones we'd seen. Maybe you had to actually be in the room before you saw what it really was. Or maybe all the things we'd seen last night were just illusions. We were dealing with alien technology. Who knew?

When we entered the Spider Café, it was full of good smells. We'd barely sat down at the counter when Mr. Moppit emerged from the kitchen carrying platters of eggs and bacon and pancakes. He was right—he did know what we wanted to eat.

The food was really good, and all four of us ate a lot more than usual. I tried to catch Mr. Moppit's eye, to confirm that we shared a secret, but I never could do it. He was too busy being the perfect waiter and the perfect chef.

When breakfast was over, Dad paid the bill and

left a nice tip. Mr. Moppit offered to show us his latest exhibit.

"I need to get to work on my car," Dad said.

"Oh, I wouldn't worry about that," Mr. Moppit assured him. "Come on. You'll be amazed."

Dad stood and threw his hands into the air. "All right," he said. "Amaze me. Come on, gang."

"Could it be?" Rocky whispered to me as we all walked over to the roadside attraction.

I shrugged. But I knew Rocky was right.

Mr. Moppit unlocked the roadside attraction and let us in. He ushered us toward a display case on the far side of the room. He'd pushed all the other exhibits a lot closer together, and in the space he'd made he'd laid out the cocoon containing Mashy Neblick.

"This is a genuine alien," he said as he opened the top of the case. "It's wrapped in genuine superhero spider silk."

"Uh-huh," Dad said. Mom just folded her arms.

"Touch it," Mr. Moppit said. "You'll see that it's real."

"I don't—"

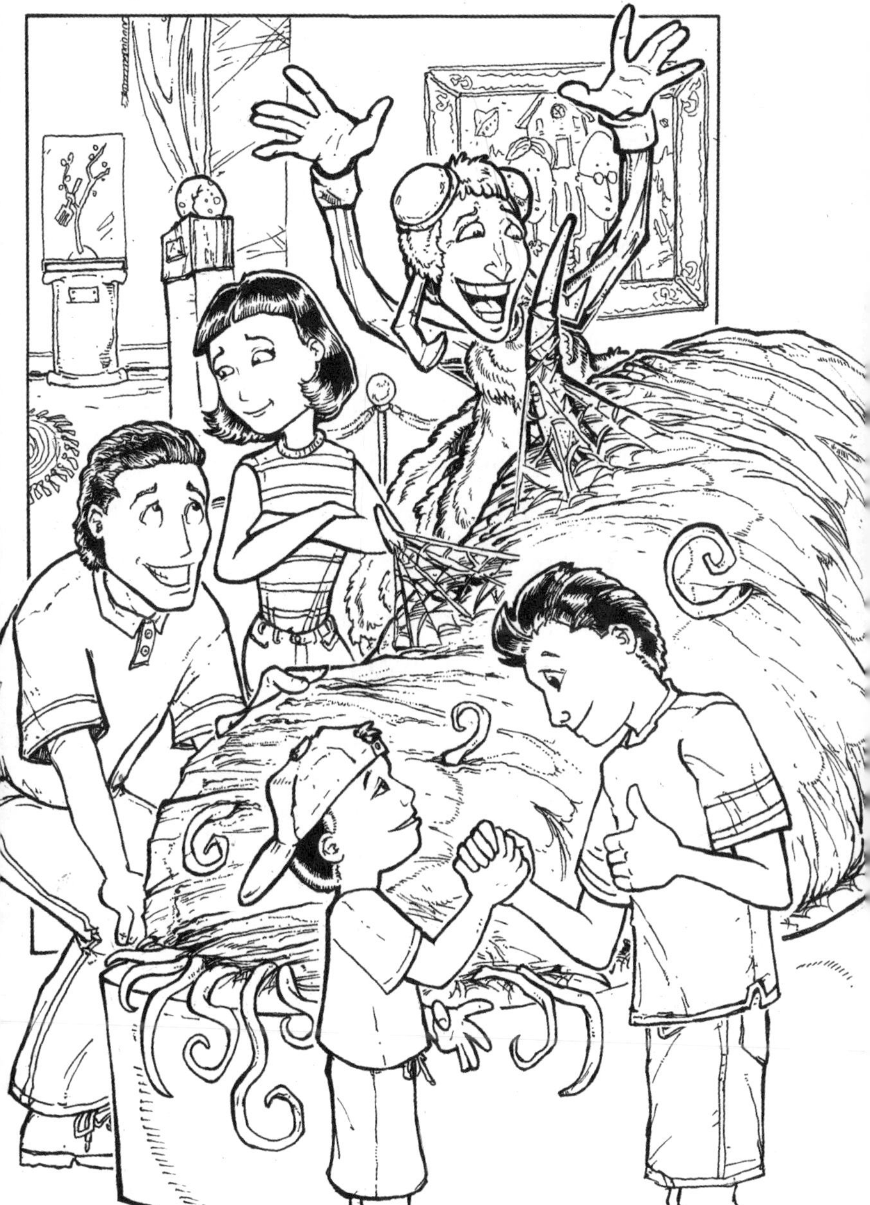

"Go ahead."

Dad poked the cocoon with one finger. "Very nice," he said. "I have to go fix the car now."

"Oh, I wouldn't worry about that," Mr. Moppit assured him for the second time that morning. He was a lot more confident about my abilities as a mechanic than I was.

"Obviously fake," Dad whispered to Mom as Mr. Moppit led the way back to the car. Mom nodded. Somehow, Dad's opinion took a load off my mind.

We all stood around while Dad got into the car and tried to start it. The engine turned over immediately. Beaming, Dad leaped from the car.

"Hurray!" Rocky cried. "We're not going to die in the desert!"

"There ya go," Dad said. "It must have been vapor lock. All it needed was to sit for a few hours."

"I guess," Mom said, sounding unsure, but also not wanting to look a gift horse in the mouth.

"You were right," Dad said to Mr. Moppit. "I didn't have to worry."

Everybody laughed.

We loaded the car. Everyone shook hands with Mr. Moppit.

"Will you be all right out here all by yourself?" Mom asked him.

"Absolutely," Mr. Moppit said. "Just the thing for me. Have a safe drive to Phoenix."

We piled into the car. Dad started it right up again, and once more we were heading east. I briefly showed the spider in slime to Rocky, and he grinned.

"Did we ever tell Mr. Moppit where we were going?" Mom asked.

"Maybe," Dad said. "Where else would we be going on this road? What difference does it make?"

Mom and Dad continued to banter as we rolled along. It was nice that things were back to normal again. And normal is how they'd stay—at least until Rocky and I got around to trying another little experiment with a certain spider in slime.

CHILLER THRILLERS™

If you're brave enough, pick up Book 2 in this series!

ATTACK OF THE LEAPING LIZARD

When Jake Johnson heard about the Crispy Crunchy Cocoa-Flakes Win-a-Bike Sweepstakes, it sounded like the contest of his dreams. Little did he realize that it would turn into his **WORST NIGHTMARE!** Who would have ever imagined that a few ordinary toy **LIZARDS** from a cereal box could suddenly turn into a living, breathing army of miniature monsters, capable of **WREAKING HAVOC** on the entire Johnson household? Can Jake outwit the **TERRIFYING** toys and save his family?

CHILLER THRILLERS™

ATTACK OF THE LEAPING LIZARD

WRITTEN BY LINDA WILLIAMS ABER   ILLUSTRATED BY DAVID ROE

$14.99 U.S.
Price higher in Canada